SAM CRESCENT

EVERNIGHT PUBLISHING ®

www.evernightpublishing.com

Copyright© 2019

Sam Crescent

Editor: Karyn White

Cover Art: Jay Aheer

ISBN: 978-0-3695-0110-3

SAM CRESCENT

THE BIKER'S NANNY

The Nannies, 3

Sam Crescent

Copyright © 2018

Chapter One

"Putting that whore to ground was the best thing I ever did," Hawk Dark said, even as his nine-month-old baby girl screamed. He didn't know what else to fucking do. He'd changed her shitty diaper. How could a baby release so much crap? He'd fed her. Burped her. Hugged her, and he wasn't going to get any sleep tonight. She just wasn't settling down.

"What about right now?" his club brother and VP, Bear, asked. He leaned up against the doorframe to the nursery.

"Especially right now. Bitch was a traitor."

"Should you be swearing like that in front of her?"

"It's not like she can fucking tell."

Bear held his hands up. "She'd be able to deal with this problem and you could get your dick wet."

"Seriously, shut the fuck up."

"Don't you have, like … Prospects for this?"

"This is my little girl. I'm not going to leave her alone with just anyone." He'd been tempted to, but seeing as he happened to love his baby girl, he wasn't about to let just anyone take care of her.

He knew how shit the world was, and he wasn't going to allow anything to hurt his baby. She'd be protected, which was why he removed her mother from the equation. She'd been ready to sell club secrets, and no one put anything before the Satan's Rulers MC, not in his club. No one betrayed his club.

They were loyal 'til death.

There was no way out.

She'd crossed a line, and no matter how much she begged, she'd ended up six feet under. Now though, he had to deal with a screaming kid, and that just wasn't good.

"Why don't you come in here and help a guy out?"

"Exactly how would I do that?"

"I don't know. Taking her for five minutes so I can take a leak."

"Nope, not happening. I've heard those things are like a virus. They spread faster than wildfire, and I have no interest in being a daddy."

"Then why are you here?"

"To go over the plans for the next run, but you're not going to be able to make it. You're going to have to find someone to take care of her, or order one of the women at the club."

Hawk thought about the club whores that were always hanging around. Some of them were good women. Had a lot of kids of their own but they weren't exactly motherly. Most days he saw them screwing one club member or all of them. Trains were pretty popular at the club, and some of the whores just loved to get fucked. They didn't even have to be one after the other. A couple of the women just loved to have all their holes filled and even wanted it uploaded onto the internet.

Whatever was a person's kink, it was completely up to them.

He wanted nothing to do with any of that. His ass was not going to be viewed on some cheap porn site for all to see.

"Not happening," Hawk said.

"You're saying that a lot. You're going to have to cave or something. A babysitter. A nanny? A fucking foster family."

"I'm not giving up my kid, and if you were anyone else, Bear, I'd fucking shoot you."

"Yeah, yeah, you tell me that all the time. I'm out of here. Enjoy your … baby."

He heard Bear leave and looked at his screaming daughter. Her face was red, and tears ran down her cheeks.

She was the first child he'd ever had. At forty-five years old, he was finally a daddy. The woman who'd given him that honor he despised, but he couldn't have everything he wanted.

"We're going to get through this. I'll figure something out."

Her cries faded to a whimper as he started to hum. Carrying her downstairs, he locked the front door, then went to the back door where he locked that as well.

Being the Prez of the Satan's Rulers MC didn't exactly offer him a lot of protection. He pissed off a lot of people and normally he was fine with that, but he didn't want to take any chances with his little girl.

"So, we're going to have to figure out what to do now. It's just the two of us, and believe me, you'll hate me for taking out your momma but one day you'll thank me. She was a no-good waste of air. She just left you home all day anyway. Yeah, I found that out. She'd leave you in your crib, then come home and pretend she'd been here all day. One of the Prospects at the club let me in on her game, so one day I came home and found you all by yourself. You were crying so bad. Worse than you are now." He sighed. His voice had taken on a playful tone. If his boys could see him now, they'd all be fucking laughing at him.

As the hour rolled on, Bethany slowly fell asleep, and he hummed to her, sitting in the living room with her resting against his chest.

Grabbing his cell phone, he took a quick selfie, wanting to remember this moment for when she was a pain-in-the-ass teenager.

He wasn't going to let her go near boys, or have anything to do with them. She was going to stay the pristine little virgin.

Finally relaxing, he closed his eyes and hoped that she didn't wake up any time soon. He had lost track of the last time he'd actually slept for more than an hour or two.

She was going to be the death of him.

He tensed up as she wriggled, her hands moving on his chest. He waited to see if she'd woken up, but she didn't. She let out a sigh, and sleep once again had hold of her.

Breathing out a sigh of relief, he closed his eyes and let sleep claim him.

****

The following morning Hawk sat in his clubhouse kitchen, drinking some nasty coffee and eating rubbery pancakes. Casey, for all of her talents with her mouth, couldn't cook for shit, but at least she tried.

Bethany had allowed him to have three hours' sleep last night and that was a world record. He was starving and tired.

"You know, you could use one of those nanny services."

"I've seen the shit that some of those nannies do," Red said from down the table. He was his soldier at arms and another man he trusted with his life. "You're better giving your daughter to a pack of wolves."

"They're not all bad. Besides, some places actually vet the women or men that come here."

"It'll have to be a girl," Hawk said, finishing off his pancake and quickly taking a swallow of his coffee as the food seemed to scratch his throat on the way down.

"How come?" Casey asked.

"It's too much of a clash. We don't need him trying to prove shit to us," Hawk said.

"Seriously? What if she responds better to guy nannies?" Casey pointed at his daughter.

"Not going to happen."

"I can't believe you're being sexist."

"I want a woman to care for my kid, not a dude. How is that sexist?"

"Because you believe taking care of kids is women's work. Don't even try to tell me differently. I've heard you say it one too many times."

"What can I say? I think women have different places in this world. The kitchen is one of them, for the kids."

Casey rolled her eyes. "You won't be getting any blowjobs any time soon."

"Again, for me, that is a woman's job."

Casey was tapping away at her mobile, and suddenly it dinged. "You're very welcome, by the way. They're the best service around. I know because my sister needed one, and she totally raved about them."

"What was wrong with your sister having them?" Bear asked.

"She and her hubby needed some time alone, and seeing as he didn't like me taking care of his kids, they organized a nanny for the entire week. It was so good she decided to stay with them."

"Yeah, 'cause he's not banging the nanny," Red said.

"No, he's not."

"Please, all guys bang the nanny," Bear said. "They're young and want to have a daddy to teach them how things go."

"You're fucking gross," Hawk said.

"Come on, Hawk, you're telling me you wouldn't bang your nanny?" Red asked.

"I won't bang any woman that's taking care of my kid."

"Okay, I've got to have a wager on this," Red said. "Bear, you in?"

"On if Hawk will bang the nanny. I'm not parting with my money until I see the nanny. She could have missing teeth, stink, and have a cackle for a laugh. Not doing that shit. I know Hawk, and he's picky about who he has on his dick."

None of them mentioned Bethany's mother.

That had been an accident, but he wasn't in the habit of sleeping with vermin. Not anymore.

"You can bet all you want. It's not going to happen."

"Just try the number. Even if she's able to get Bethany down at night, I'm sure it'll be worth it."

****

Jasmine Clark had a meeting in two hours. She had to get some groceries, head to the post office, and of course make sure she wore something presentable as she'd been asked to go on an interview. Not her personally. She worked for an agency that had nannies in four different areas. Those nannies that had finished a job or been let go had gotten the notification, and seeing as she was nearest to the proposed job, then she'd been the one to be asked.

She didn't know who it was for, only the where.

That was another thing; her GPS was totally down, so now she was having to use a good old out-of-date map to find the location. She lived close, but not that close to where her next job was. She was running so behind.

This was why she should never ever drop toys off at the children's wing of the hospital. Time just sucked right out of her, and now she was running behind. The bank was going to have to be on the list of things to do today. She may not even make it to the post office as it was only open half a day on Wednesdays.

"Come on, Jasmine. You've got this."

She ran through the produce department and passed the meat section. Deciding against beef, she grabbed some chicken for half-price; so yay, freeze some for later. She'd just gone down the section for baking when she heard a whimper and then a cry. Babies crying always broke her heart and not for any reason other than she hated to hear babies cry. It was the worst thing in the world.

Well, maybe not the worst thing, but it was something she couldn't stand.

Rounding the aisle, she came to a stop when she saw a huge man bending over looking at different kinds of baby food and diapers.

He wore one of those MC cuts, but from the look of it, it wasn't merchandise from a TV show. This was the real deal.

MCs were all violent, weren't they?

She didn't know many of them.

She froze as he lifted a hand and placed it on the baby, softly shushing the sound. The baby didn't like that.

Jasmine expected him to lose his temper or something like that as the baby wasn't doing what he wanted. Instead, he stood and smiled at the baby.

Slowly walking past, she offered him a smile.

"I'm sorry for the noise," he said, his voice dark and deep.

She nibbled her lip and shrugged. "It can't be helped most of the time. Boy or girl?" she asked.

The baby suit was white and she could never tell the sex in neutral colors, not that it mattered.

"This is a girl. Bethany. She's a screamer."

"You've got to shop too. She's so adorable."

"You really think that when she's crying."

"I'm weird. I find kids, puppies, dogs, rabbits, and rainbows beautiful."

"Not kittens?"

"Oh, them too, but I didn't want to sound too weird." She chuckled. "You have got a beautiful set of lungs on you." She smiled at Bethany.

Slowly, as if by some miracle, Bethany's cries stopped, and she watched her.

"Wow, okay, I'm taking you back with me because that is some miracle you've worked there. How the fuck did you do that?"

"I don't know. I love kids."

"Do you have your own?" he asked.

A sharp pain slashed through her heart. "No, I don't have any babies of my own. I've not been that lucky."

"That is the first time she's been quiet all day."

"Would you like me to, I don't know, stand with her while you shop? Would you like that?"

"You'd do that?" he asked.

"Sure, I've not got anything else to do." She could do the post office another day and she can finish off her shopping.

"You can put your stuff into my cart, and we can separate it." He lifted up a huge chunk of beef and placed it down the middle. "See?"

"I'll be back." She put her few items in her section, took her trolley back, and then returned to find him waiting.

"The name's Hawk."

"Jasmine."

"Jasmine?"

"Yeah, my mom loved the name, so she wanted me to have it." She gave a shrug.

"It's a pretty name."

She was not some schoolgirl that wasn't used to taking a compliment. At thirty years old she'd met her fair share of charmers.

"I really like Bethany."

"Yeah, me too."

"Where's your wife or your girlfriend?" *Real smooth, Jasmine. Just go right ahead and find his marital status?* She didn't even know why she was curious. It's not like she was interested in the guy.

He was a biker.

She wouldn't have anything to do with bikes.

Bikes were not her thing. Gripping the trolley, she followed Hawk down the aisle, picking up some chocolate chips and vanilla and putting them in her section of the trolley. She had a baking addiction, and it was her mission that every time she baked, she did something a bit different. This week she intended to make peanut butter brownies. *Yum.* Just the sound of it put on ten pounds, not that she minded at all.

She'd long given up on worrying about being a slender woman. At a size eighteen, she was more than happy with her figure.

From a young age she'd had to deal with large tits and hips, along with thick, chunky thighs. She was done with all kinds of diets. She'd tried most of them, failed them all. Dieting held no interest to her.

Five years ago, she'd learned the hard way that life can take unexpected turns and that it was only a short time they were here on earth. She intended to live her life to the fullest. The only thing missing was sex.

Glancing toward the man on her right, who looked relieved to have his little girl quiet, she wondered what he was like in bed.

"I don't have one," he said after a long pause.

It was on the tip of her tongue to ask him why, but she held herself back. She didn't want to make a fool of herself and just ask him to fuck her.

Not that she'd ever be able to ask him that.

She dreamed about it though.

Imagined and fantasized about what it would be like to have a man worship her. To take her, to use her, to fuck her. Part of her wanted to be treated like a whore, to be well and truly taken but afterward to be held. That was something she was never going to have, so she decided to use her trusty fingers and a very good imagination. She'd even tried porn a few times, but that didn't do it for her.

She tried not to laugh at some of the scenes she'd watched, but she was sure she saw one of the women making a list in between being taken in the ass and pussy. There was just nothing there for her to enjoy in that kind of lovemaking. What was the appeal with that kind of stuff?

They made their way down to canned soup section; she just loved cream of mushroom and cream of celery. They worked wonders in casseroles if she didn't have the chance to make it from scratch. There was only so much she could make after coming home from a really long day.

She pushed the trolley with her arms while she let Bethany play with her fingers. The little girl kept squeezing them. She wanted to ask more questions about her mother and stuff like that but decided against it.

Once they rang up their purchases, they made their way out to the car.

Hawk followed her to hers and then she helped him by putting Bethany in the car seat as he loaded up his truck.

She closed the door as quietly as she could.

"Thank you for that. It's been some time since I was able to think while shopping."

"No problem. I was happy to help. You've got a beautiful daughter." She shook his hand and felt completely weird about doing that.

It wasn't a shaking of the hand kind of deal or anything other than being nice.

"Have a nice day." She pulled her hand back and walked away. Glancing over her shoulder once, she saw him staring back at her.

Caught looking at him, she bit her lip but couldn't help but smile. She liked that look in his eyes, especially as she was kind of into him too.

But there was no "kind of" about it.

She was into him.

If she didn't have a job to go to this afternoon she may have even asked for his phone number.

Don't be crazy. He's a damn biker.
Totally out of your league.
She could dream though.

Hawk would be featuring in a couple of her dreams.

Chapter Two

"Do you really think it's the right thing to do to have your nanny come here?" Casey asked.

The club whore sat down beside him. Bethany sat on his knee, holding his hands, and wasn't screaming about anything.

"I don't want anyone at my place. Not unless I know for sure that I can trust them. It's too dangerous, and I wouldn't put her in harm's way."

"This isn't about being in harm's way. Some women are put off by the lifestyle," Casey said. "They'll not work for you."

"I checked the company out. They're legit. Their nannies have never had a criminal offense against them, and they don't employ pervs. I'd say that's pretty damn good," Bear said, taking a seat.

Several of the guys were hanging around. They were probably waiting for the fresh meat to enter the club. Whoever the woman was, she'd better have a strong stomach as the boys wanted some new pussy hanging around.

What Hawk hoped for when this nanny came around was someone who waved a magic wand over his daughter and was immune to the biker life. The last thing he wanted was a woman that preferred to spend time riding dick rather than taking care of his girl.

He thought about the cute little blonde he saw this morning. He'd noticed her rounding the aisle and even notice his screaming kid. At first, he'd thought she was going to tell him to take care of his girl better. Instead, she'd given him a sweet as fuck smile that made him think about showing her all the dirty things he could do with her mouth, and then offered to help. What guy would turn her down?

She wasn't part of this lifestyle, not even close. She'd worn a summery dress with flowers on it and a cardigan over her shoulders. Her blonde hair had been pulled up on top of her head, and she was completely void of makeup. She'd looked like a fifties-style mother who cooked pancakes or waffles for breakfast. He wasn't into that.

That was a lie.

He'd been totally into that, but seeing as he had a daughter and a club to deal with, fucking anything but a club whore wouldn't work. He wasn't after any commitments. Just easy sex where he didn't even have to think about anything.

All it needed to be was mechanical.

Bethany gurgled, and he kissed the top of her head, not caring one bit what his club thought of him for showing affection to his girl.

"Boss, any idea what this woman looks like that's coming to an interview?" Red asked.

"Nope. Not a chance. She'll have an ID card. Clark, something Clark. I didn't quite catch the first name," he said.

"Look at that ass. Damn, I'd love to spread those juicy cheeks and show her just how good it would be to be fucked by me," Brick said.

Several of his men looked out of the window, but the way he was sitting he couldn't even catch a glimpse of the woman they were all staring at.

"Those tits, man, she could take a cock."

"Don't ever fall for a guy that speaks like that," Hawk said, whispering against his daughter's ear. "Use all of them to find out what you should or shouldn't be looking for in a man."

"Hawk, man, you may want to find a new nanny. This one has 'fuck me' all over her."

"Behave. Casey, go and check her ID and make sure she's the right woman," Hawk said. "All of you, sit down and pretend to be human men and not fucking vultures."

"Wait until you see her," Red said. "You're going to want to fuck her."

Rolling his eyes, he saw a couple of the whores were looking at the door like they wanted to murder whoever came through.

He moved Bethany onto the other knee, and she started whimpering and he immediately placed her on the other. She tried to wriggle in his grasp. There was a carpeted area in his office that he put down for her but not in the main clubroom. Anything could be on the floor, and seeing as sleeping was a pastime at the moment, he didn't intend to encourage his daughter to crawl through God knows what that decorated the floor. He paid a good company, but he knew for a fact there was only so much filth they could get up.

Forensics would have a field day with the floor.

"Hawk, your guest is here." Casey walked over to him, taking a seat. He looked behind her and the woman his men had been panting and drooling over was none other than the cute blonde at the grocery store.

"Hawk?"

"Jasmine?"

"You two know each other?" Casey asked.

"Hardly," Jasmine said. "I … I helped him grocery shop. This little one wouldn't let him concentrate for a second."

"You're from the nanny agency."

"Yes." She showed him her ID and sure enough, Jasmine Clark. "I've also got several references for you to look at." She handed him an envelope. "They're all in there if you'd like to check them out."

"Why don't you take a seat?" he said, taking the envelope from her.

"I had no idea this was where I was going to be coming, otherwise I'd have done my interview at the grocery store."

"Your agency only told me your name was Ms. Clark."

"It's Miss Clark. I'm no longer married, and Clark's my maiden name. I dropped his after the divorce." She ran her hands down her dress.

It was different from the one she wore at the store but no less feminine. This one enhanced her large tits and flared hips.

He was paying too much attention to her body and not to her references.

"Have you been a nanny for long?" Casey asked.

"Over five years now. I was a nanny in my early twenties for a few years, but once I married, I stopped and focused on him. After our divorce I went back to nannying, only there've been a few positions that don't require a live-in, so I've gone to their house every day and taken care of their babies, then come home at the end of the day."

"This position will be live-in," Hawk said. "My hours are … random. I won't be able to give you a schedule."

"That's fine. I can make arrangements to rent out my apartment. I offer a month's notice to any tenant when I need to move back in. If you consider me could we include a month's notice for termination of my employment?"

"There will be conditions that would bring that termination forward."

"Such as?" she asked.

"If I find out you're hurting my daughter." Not

only would he kill her but it would also bring about immediate termination.

The look of absolute disgust took him away.

"I would never hurt a child. Never. I have scolded a child for doing wrong, but that is at the parent's permission. I would never dream of ever hurting a child at all."

"Fine. Fine. Just so we're on the same page."

"We are. I swear. If you consider me, I'll take good care of your little girl."

He tried to get comfortable with Bethany in his arms and read the references, but it wasn't working. "Are you good to take her while I read through these?"

"Certainly." Jasmine took Bethany, turning her so that the little girl's back was to her chest. Her arm was across her stomach and Bethany gave a little giggle, content to sit on her lap.

He watched them for a few minutes.

Jasmine looked so calm with his daughter. She held her hand out and Bethany grasped her fingers, squeezing them and tugging at them as if they were sausages or something.

Looking away, he checked out her references and saw a couple of the names he recognized from around town. Wealthy families with lots of kids. They had glowing reports, and he read a brief description. She'd been taking care of children from babies through to eighteen where not only did she help them with their extracurricular activities, she helped with study class and college applications.

He needed someone like her to look after his little girl.

She was too busy concentrating on his daughter, not giving his club the time of day. The boys were watching her. They were like a pack of hungry wolves, ready to devour their prey. He had a feeling there was way more to Jasmine than met the eye.

"How about we take this into my office?" he asked.

"Sure. Bethany's coming too?"

"Yes."

"Excellent."

She looked good with a kid in her arms.

Why was he thinking about her and kids like that? He had to get his head on straight.

He took the lead, showing her through to his office. Glancing behind her, he saw several of the guys holding their dicks. He couldn't believe some of them were supposed to be full-grown men and were acting like immature children.

Closing the door, he took a seat behind his desk as she sat on the opposite side. If he took her as his nanny, she'd be at his home, around him all the time, and he wouldn't be able to touch her.

Fuck.

His luck wasn't with him today.

****

Jasmine wanted the job.

She didn't want the job.

When she'd parked up outside of the Satan's Rulers MC clubhouse she figured it was a big old coincidence.

She should have known better.

Luck was never on her side, and looking at the man now, there was no way she'd be able to actually live her fantasy. She'd only met him a few hours ago, but she'd found herself daydreaming about him anyway.

"You're good with kids. Good with her."

"I hope you believe me when I say I didn't have a clue that you were you and that I'd be meeting you this afternoon."

He held his hand up. "No problem. I didn't know it was you. I didn't catch your first name that the woman told me over the phone."

"Oh."

"Yeah, it was just one of those things. Meeting at the grocery store. You helped me out a lot today already. I would understand if you don't want to proceed with this interview."

"Why wouldn't I want to proceed?" she asked.

"The club." He tapped his patch.

"Your club has nothing to do with taking care of a little girl."

"Being at my place you're going to see a lot of club brothers there. We do business there and here at the club."

"Will it be dangerous?"

"I try not to let my professional life touch my private life."

That wasn't exactly an answer, but she got the general gist. He couldn't guarantee it wouldn't hit at his home, but he did everything to make sure it didn't. She'd heard plenty around town about the Satan's Rulers MC. They liked to party hard. Several of the places had been torn up pretty bad because of their hard partying. Fights breaking out, brawls, arguments, and then just plain vandalism.

Spending most of her time around kids, she'd not seen any of it in person.

Bethany snuggled in and, glancing down at the young child, Jasmine saw she was going to sleep.

"You really don't have any children of your own?"

"No, I don't. Erm, I would still like to be considered for the position."

"You're the only one that has agreed to a meeting."

"I am?"

"Yes, I've had three people lined up before you, and all three of them cancelled even before they got through the door."

"Wow, I'm sure it had nothing to do with your club."

"It has everything to do with my club, but I'm not offended. I know this place isn't for everyone, and that's their loss. I'm not going to change for her. She'll live with being a biker's daughter. Simple as."

"So, what are the arrangements you're hoping for?" she asked.

"A live-in position. That part is not negotiable. If you're requiring any vacations or days off, I will need to be notified in advance. I will also need to know of any boyfriends or friends you want hanging around."

"No boyfriends?"

"Lovers?"

"None," she said.

"Really?"

"Do you find that hard to believe?"

He leaned back and smiled. "I do."

"There's no one, Mr. Dark."

"Call me Hawk."

"Hawk, is there anything else?"

"We have family get-togethers. Other clubs come and join in the fun. I'm going to need you here for those to keep an eye on Bethany. You're not allowed to date any of the club brothers while you're in my employment, or even to date. If you decide to date someone outside of the club, I want to vet him first."

"Wow," she said. "That's a very strange arrangement."

"My kid, my rules."

"Okay. I can handle that." It wasn't like she was dating anyone right now. She tried to think back to the last date, and it had to be well over a year now since that disaster. She'd been content to be on her own.

"Yeah, I want you to start immediately. Will that be a problem?"

Staring down at the little girl, she couldn't help but smile. Who could resist such a charming child? "I've got no problem with that."

"Awesome. How do we do this?"

"If you call the agency they will handle all the details and contract and stuff. I'm going to at least pack a few things. Would that be okay?"

She stood up and her heart melted as Bethany snuggled in against her.

"Will I be meeting her mother?"

"Her mother's dead."

"Oh, I'm so sorry."

"Don't be. I'm not. The woman was a waste of space. We'll come with you. I came in my car so we can get your stuff and then I'll take you to my place."

"You don't need to do that. I can pack something and drive to your place if you give me the directions."

"Not happening. Another condition is you're going to have to do as I tell you."

"I'm not a child."

"My house. My baby. My rules."

She stared at him. She hated to admit it, but she was a little turned on by the fact that he had his rules and was taking charge.

"Fine. I just didn't want to put you out of your way."

"You won't." He grabbed the baby bag.

A biker with a baby bag was the hottest thing

she'd seen all year. He wore his leather cut, but there was no denying his thick muscles.

She normally didn't go for a guy with a beard, but his made him look ruggedly handsome. Dangerous. Deadly.

Get a grip.

Following him out of his office, she saw several of his members waiting. Some of the women were pretty much naked, walking around in their underwear. She was sure she saw a guy being serviced by one of the women in the back of the club.

Note to self. Buy sanitizer for whenever she visited the club, not that she'd be visiting it often.

This wasn't a social call.

She put Bethany into the car seat and climbed into the back.

Hawk didn't question her as she settled in, buckling her seatbelt. She was a little nervous at how she reacted around him.

He was the first man in a long time that she couldn't seem to … ignore. Pushing some hair off her face, she glanced out of the window, trying her hardest not to look back at him, even though she really wanted to.

Every now and then, she looked toward him, wondering what he was thinking.

"We'll have to take those groceries with us," he said. "Some of them would spoil."

"Yes, they will."

She'd never been good at conversation.

It was one of the reasons she loved spending time with kids. They were happy to talk about anything. The movies they watched. The food they ate. The bubbles they made in the garden, or even the fact they went to the potty.

She never talked about her bathroom breaks with anyone.

There were limits to what she would share.

"Do you have any other children?" she asked.

"None. Bethany is all I have. Have you always taken care of kids?"

"Yes. When I was married I worked in a nursery, but for the most part I've been a nanny. I love it. I love looking after children."

Fortunately, the journey wasn't that long, and as he parked up, she opened her door.

"I'll be down in a minute."

She rushed up the flight of stairs to her own apartment. Her hands shook a little as she opened up her door.

This was a new chapter in her life.

She was going to be a nanny for a biker.

It was a little surreal.

A lot surreal, actually.

Especially as she was having some dirty thoughts about said biker.

Throwing some clothes into a suitcase, she grabbed the perishables into a couple of bags and closed the door behind her. She'd come back and get the other stuff she'd need. The furniture came with her apartment, and as she'd be renting it out, she wouldn't need to worry about it.

Making her way down to the car, she saw Hawk standing outside the car, smoking a cigarette.

"That was fast."

"I'll have to come back for the rest. I have what I need."

"I'll get one of the boys to help with that," he said. "You don't have to worry about a thing."

Why did she have a feeling that her life was about

to change forever?

Chapter Three

One month later

Hawk spent way too much time at home already. It was a Friday night, and rather than be at the club fucking one of the number of club whores that wanted him, he was parked in his driveway.

He already spotted Jasmine's car, and in the backseat was his daughter's chair. The first week she moved in, she asked him to help fix that thing in her car. It was a massive one, but it meant a quick glance in her rearview mirror and she'd be able to see Bethany. A couple of the boys had seen her in town, and even though she didn't acknowledge them, they all spoke very highly of her.

She took care of his daughter as if she was his own, her kindness showing through in every passing second.

He'd even put a few cameras around his home to check on her to make sure he wasn't getting the wrong vibe off her. It had been easy to do, and now any time he wanted, he could check in at home through his cell phone and she didn't even know that he was checking up on her. Each time he did, she was either playing with Bethany, feeding her, cleaning, cooking, or something that a wife would do.

It was like having a wife, only he didn't get to fuck her—and he really wanted to. Coming home every single night wasn't about getting her home-cooked food, which in itself was like heaven on a plate. No, he went home every night because he liked being in her company. She didn't make demands on him. They hung out, watched movies, talked about everything and anything. She never asked about the club or what he was doing. If she didn't see him for days at a time, she didn't expect an explanation. He would tell her if he'd be gone a few days but again, no questions or curiosity as to why. Just simple acceptance of it.

Climbing off his bike, he made his way inside and was once again met with the most amazing smell.

"I think that's Daddy, baby girl. I think he's come to see you. Let's hope he likes your surprise."

He walked down the short corridor and entered the kitchen where he found an apron-covered Jasmine and his little girl in her high chair. Bethany had some toys, and Jasmine was covered in flour.

"Hey, you're home. You're a bit early."

"What are you making?"

"We're making pizza. We've already done some chocolate chip and walnut cookies. They're over there cooling if you'd like one. My pizza sauce is ready, and now I'm just shaping my pizza." She held a ball of dough in her hand.

"That's a lot of pizzas you got there." He did a quick count and discovered ten already made and cooling on trays.

"Yes. Life can get pretty hectic, and I've been making food that can go straight from freezer to oven. That way I don't have to worry."

"You could order out."

"That I could but I know how to make myself some pizza and tomorrow it will be lasagna. I've already cleaned every surface in this place, and Bethany loves seeing me in the kitchen. I think she likes it here."

Since Jasmine had been living with him in the spare bedroom, he'd enjoyed a whole month of full nights' sleeps.

He'd not even heard his little girl wake up.

"I'm sorry to ask this, does she wake up in the night?"

"The first week I was here, she did. I'd change her diaper, feed her, burp her, and then just rock her for a few minutes before putting her back to sleep. We do so much during the day now that she's too tired to wake up. Why?"

"I just, I could never get her to sleep before you came along. She'd be awake and that was it, she wasn't going back to sleep."

"Babies thrive on routine, but she spends a lot of time playing. I've got a little secure playpen in the living room. She can crawl around and play with her toys. She'll be walking before you know it. I've taken her out into the garden as well. If you tire her out, she'll sleep soundly at night."

Jasmine always knew what she was doing.

He didn't want just anyone taking care of his little girl, so he'd gotten a background check done on her. There were a few things about her life that she wasn't telling him. He didn't want to just blab them out or demand answers. She'd not technically lied to him. Jasmine didn't have children, but that didn't mean she hadn't been expecting one.

The thorough background check he had done made him aware that at one time she'd been pregnant. The child she'd given birth to had been stillborn. She'd had umbilical cord prolapse. Her baby had been starved of oxygen within her womb and had died. It was a rare condition. Less than a year after her loss, she'd gotten a divorce. He also knew she had to sign herself into a psychiatric ward for six months where she was evaluated because she wanted to end her own life. She'd been strong enough not to do that and to seek help. After a period of time, she released herself, and hadn't been back. She wasn't on any medication or watch list.

No cops wanted her in different states.

During that time, she'd been all alone in the world.

Her husband was long gone. Over five years now, and since then he'd married someone else and now had two children. Hawk didn't want to bring up bad memories, but he was curious about her life. Why she kept it a secret and especially now as she seemed healthier, better. He'd also gotten the full details of her employment record at the agency where he'd hired her.

In the last five years, she'd been their best employee. Her clients were nothing but happy with her, and she seemed perfectly content with her life. The first day he met her at the grocery store, she'd been happy and now she was even more so.

His curiosity was getting the better of him.

"Why didn't you tell me you were pregnant?" he asked.

This made her freeze as she was shaping the dough.

Jasmine looked up at him.

He saw the frown on her face and then her lips pressed together.

"You had a background check run on me?"

"I'm the Prez of the Satan's Rulers MC, Jasmine. I have to make sure that my daughter is well taken care of."

She looked at his little girl. She looked disappointed and even a little hurt. "You know everything then. All about my life."

"Yes. I know about your marriage. What caused it to end. The loss of your baby and your stay in a psychiatric ward," he said.

"Just because you're part of an MC doesn't give you the right to interfere with my life."

"No, but there's nothing you can do about me

finding out, so now just talk to me. I want to make sure that my daughter is okay."

"I would never harm a child."

"That may be. Why did you put yourself in a ward if you weren't worried about what you were going to do?"

She put down the dough. She wiped her hands and lifted Bethany up in her arms. "I'll be back."

He followed her through to the sitting room where she placed Bethany.

She turned toward him and stared in his eyes. "Because every single day I felt guilty that my child was dead and I was alive. For hours I'd lay in the bath, the blade poised to my wrists, and I was so close to cutting. To just letting nature take its course. I was alone. I'd divorced my husband, and I wanted everything to just … stop. I couldn't press pause. I couldn't make the feelings go away. I just wanted everything to just be quiet. I didn't want to die. I didn't want to … I don't know, ruin my shot of getting into heaven maybe. I don't know what happens on the other side."

"You're religious?"

"I'm not, but I want to think that my little boy is on the other side. That's he's happy and I can live with that. Instead of killing myself I did something that I never thought I'd do. I got the help I needed, and being in that ward for six months, I was able to press pause. People were there to help me and I was able to grieve and move on, and I got better. The pain still doesn't go away, but I can talk about him. I can think about him and know that I can take a bath and not hurt or kill myself. What you found out, Hawk, is really private. I don't tell anyone because I just don't. It's not important for everyone to know that. If you're not happy with the care I provide your daughter, then please let my agency know and I will be out of here within the month, or sooner if you're not happy. I'm also aware that my ex is happily married with kids, if that's what you're wondering as well. Not bad for a guy that apparently hadn't wanted kids with *me*."

She walked past him into the kitchen.

Now he felt like a fucking asshole.

****

Jasmine checked on Bethany to see the girl was still fast asleep. Slowly, creeping out of the room, she headed downstairs. It was five in the morning, but she couldn't sleep. Hawk's confrontation last night had taken it out of her. She'd gone through the motions, finished pizza, cleaned up, eaten, bathed Bethany, put her to bed. The moment she'd gone to her room, other than to attend Bethany last night, she'd not left her room.

She should have known something like this would happen.

The past was always out there for someone to find. She couldn't even blame Hawk for finding out the truth.

Pushing fingers through her hair, she entered the kitchen and came to a stop. Hawk was there.

Only this was a Hawk she hadn't seen.

He wore a pair of sweatpants and nothing else. The leather cut that he normally sported was nowhere in sight. His muscular, heavily inked body was on full display for her to look at. Even though she was pissed at him about last night, she couldn't stop staring at him. He looked so incredible.

Her pussy tightened, and she tried to ignore the yearning that suddenly built up inside her.

"You're awake early," he said, putting the coffee machine on.

"I couldn't sleep. I had a rough night."

"I owe you an apology."

"You don't owe me anything. You're right. I'm taking care of your little girl, and you have a right to know about what happened in my past. It's no less than what I would have done if I had a child. I didn't lie to you. I don't have any children. I just don't think it would have worked me spilling out my past to you like that. Not even at an interview. I asked the agency about what I should and shouldn't say. They were the ones to advise me that it was in the past. They are more than happy with my work." She took a deep breath and stared at the counter.

The last thing she ever wanted was for him to think that she had gone out of her way to deceive him. That's not what she wanted, not one bit.

"I'm sorry for prying into your life. I shouldn't have done it," he said. "At least, I shouldn't have told you that shit last night. I blurted it out. I was worried."

"You've got no reason to worry. I'll protect your girl with my life." She'd not been crazy when she entered that psych ward. In fact, some of the doctors had even said she didn't need to do it because she'd proven to them she wasn't going to end her life.

Jasmine hadn't been willing to take that chance.

"You're good for Bethany. Is the little angel sleeping?" Hawk asked.

"She is."

"You're a damn miracle worker, that's for sure."

"Why?"

"I couldn't get her to sleep. Her favorite thing to do was to keep me awake. I'm pushing forty-six years old, and believe me, I need my beauty sleep."

"You're looking okay to me." Her cheeks heated when she realized what she was saying. "Do you want breakfast?"

"I'd love some. I made some coffee. Not that it's any good."

She walked toward the coffee pot and poured some out. Taking a sniff, she didn't see a problem with it so proceeded to sip a small bit of the hot, dark liquid. It was incredibly bitter, and she couldn't keep the disgusted look off her face.

"I rest my case."

"I'll make breakfast and coffee from now on." She gave his shoulder a gentle squeeze, feeling the hard muscles beneath.

He was such a big man; a huge man.

She grabbed the necessary items out of the fridge, ignoring the way her pussy seemed to wake up whenever she was around him. Any kind of sexual relationship with this man would be bad. She adored Bethany, but it was also against the agency policy and they were known for stopping by for random visits. She could get fired from the company.

Being a well-respected nanny meant the world to her.

Pushing some hair off her shoulder, she chanced a glance back at him. He was looking at the newspaper that he had delivered every single day but never read. She'd collect them and put them in a neat pile next to his chair in the sitting room.

In the past month they'd become very domesticated together. He didn't mind that she cooked and baked often.

The scent of homemade cookies always made her feel safe and warm. Especially after her mother died of cancer several years ago. Her father hadn't lasted much longer after that. They had that kind of love that bound the two of them together.

With bacon and eggs ready, she got started on

making a killer breakfast. Today she was starving.

She heard a whimper from upstairs and was about to go and get Bethany when Hawk held up his hand.

"I'll get her. You carry on. I've got to eat."

Chuckling, she continued with breakfast, content to be in the kitchen. Her mother always said that a woman's place was in the kitchen. At first, she thought it was incredibly sexist, and in a way it was, but to her, it was her place. She cooked.

Her parents had that dynamic where the man went out to work and the woman stayed home, cooked, cleaned, and took care of the kids, or kid in her parents' case.

They were happy with that, and for a long time, she'd been happy keeping house for her husband. Pushing those thoughts aside, she smiled as he brought Bethany into the room.

"She's changed and happy."

"Awesome. Morning, Bethany."

The little girl made a few gurgling sounds. It wouldn't be long before she started to actually talk.

Hawk put her in the high chair and started to feed his daughter with the food she'd provided on the kitchen counter.

Finishing up their breakfast, she served them up on two plates. Joining him at the counter, she dug in as he fed the last spoonful to Bethany.

"I'm going to be gone for a couple of days in a week's time. Work stuff."

"Okay."

"If you need anything, all you got to do is stop by the club. Don't worry, they won't bite."

"I know they won't. They all seemed really nice," she said.

None of them had pulled a gun on her or tried to

hurt her. She considered that a win.

"They were on their best behavior. Don't be fooled by them though. They were saying some pretty dirty-as-fuck things about what they wanted to do to you."

"Oh, okay, well, erm, that wouldn't work at all. I told you I don't date."

"No, you don't." He kept on staring at her.

"What's wrong?"

"I've never met a woman that followed the rules. They were always intent on breaking them."

She shrugged. "I love rules. I love order, and when you break that apart it can hurt so many people. Mostly kids."

"You feel strongly about that?"

"Yeah. Kids need a balance. They need structure and rules. Boundaries. You know, that kind of stuff that helps them. You must think I'm a loser or something." She cringed. A loser? Really? Was she in high school?

"I don't think anything of the sort. It's rather refreshing to have a woman talk to me and not try to get off on my dick."

She looked into his eyes to see if he was joking.

He wasn't.

"Is that all you get? A woman trying to have sex with you?"

"Pretty much. Being Prez of an MC, it makes my tag a victory for them. To become an old lady in my world is to become queen."

"Oh."

"Yeah, oh. Women want power. I screw a woman, it goes to her head, and I've had to deal with the fallout."

"Old lady?"

"It's a term we use for our women. The ones that

have been chosen by men of the club, not anything else."

"Oh, it's not exactly a nice name."

"It's better than sweet-butt or club whore."

"Wow," she said. "Yeah, it really is." She burst out laughing. Getting to her feet, she did the dishes and left them on the drainer.

"Am I forgiven for last night?"

"You don't even have to worry about last night." She grabbed his daughter. "We're heading to the park today. Would you like to come? We feed the ducks down at the river as well. She loves that."

She saw him hesitate for a split second.

"I'd love that."

"Excellent. I'll get her ready."

She was moving across the hall when the first gunshot rang out. At first, she didn't know what it was until she heard Hawk yell for her to get down.

With the baby in her arms, she held onto Bethany, dropping to the floor as more shots rang out. She heard the smashing of windows and stuff being broken as gunshots were fired.

Hawk's home had just been shot out, and now she had pain in her shoulder. Bethany was crying, and she panicked. Glancing down at the little girl, she checked her all over and discovered she was fine. Jasmine herself, however, wasn't.

She'd been hit in the shoulder. If she'd not been carrying Bethany on her other hip, she knew without a doubt that she'd have lost her charge today. Saying a quick thank you to whoever was looking down on them, she saw Hawk enter the hallway. Pressing a hand to her shoulder, she gave him a watery smile as the pain had exploded. "Bethany's fine."

Chapter Four

Bethany's fine.

Not, "I've been shot."

No. "Bethany's fine."

Hawk was fucking raging as he watched the doctor look over Jasmine's wound. His boys had arrived ten minutes fucking late after his home was hit in a drive-by. Some piece of shit thought they could attack his home.

They hadn't hit him. He'd gotten his gun and fired back. He had the license plate and he was going to find that piece of shit and then there was going to be some blood. No one fired on his home. Bethany could have been hit. Jasmine *was* fucking hit. She winced as the doctor injected some painkiller into her shoulder. The bullet was there.

"I need to go to the hospital," she said. "Please, can I go to the hospital?"

Tears fell from her eyes, and it was breaking his heart to see her like this.

Bear was on the other side and even his VP was having a hard time watching her. They had all been shot a time or two. Even a few club whores, but they'd take whatever the doctor or the club needed to shut them the fuck up for him to do his job.

Jasmine wasn't a club whore.

She wasn't going to take some drug to keep herself high.

The doctor patted her arm and turned to him. Bear and Red came in close as they were there.

"I've numbed the area, but she's moving too much. I need to get that bullet. I'm going to have to knock her out or you're going to need to hold her down while I do this," the doctor said.

Stepping forward, he put his hands on Jasmine's thighs. She still wore the pajamas she'd come downstairs in.

"Jasmine, you can't go to the hospital."

"They have doctors and hospital beds and people who can do this without causing me pain."

"Baby, I hate to say this, but this guy here is a damn good doctor. He's stitched all of us up. I'm not going to let anything happen to you."

In the distance they heard Bethany screaming.

"I've got to go and help her," Jasmine said.

"She's fine. What you need to do is get fixed right now."

"I want to go to the hospital."

"If you're wanting to get knocked out, I can give you a little something and it'll take the pain right away," Bear said.

"No. I don't want that."

"The pain isn't going to go away until you let me take care of it," the doctor said.

Jasmine was strong.

He, Bear, and Red were stronger.

"How long?" he asked.

"A few minutes and then I can stitch her up."

He nodded his head. There was no way she was going to the hospital. All gunshot wounds had to be reported, which meant cops. They'd been riding their ass trying to get into the club for fucking years. He wasn't about to have a cop in his place, nor was he going to let the motherfucker who did this get away with it.

Staring into Jasmine's eyes, he gave the signal for Bear and Red. They all knew what to do. They've done it before.

"Jasmine, do you trust me not to let anything happen to you?" he asked.

"Yes, why?" He'd moved away to the top of the makeshift bed that they had in the basement.

"Good." He grabbed her shoulders, making sure not to touch her wound, and drawing her back on the bed.

"What are you doing?"

Bear took her waist, and Red took her feet.

The doctor approached.

"No. Please. I want to go to the hospital. No. No. No." She screamed as the doctor got to work. It was a matter of moments because he was so damn good, but her screams seemed to go on forever. Her strength was no match for him, Bear, and Red. They held her in place without so much as a wriggle as the doctor pulled out the bullet. Still holding her down, the doctor stitched her up and then gave her the injection that put her to sleep.

Her screams ceased, and slowly, she slumped into sleep.

He hoped she wasn't in any kind of pain.

"Why the fuck didn't you give her that?" Bear asked, looking a little shaken.

"I couldn't. I needed to make sure she wasn't going into shock while I pulled the bullet. She had no signs of shock as I withdrew it or when I stitched her up. I don't have any monitors to make sure she's stable. Someone will need to stay with her while she's under. I figure you'd prefer her like this than awake after that," the doctor said. "My fee is the same. Please offer my apologies to her."

The doctor left, and Hawk didn't wait a single moment. He picked her up in his arms and carried her out of the basement.

Red and Bear followed behind him.

No one said a word as she carried her upstairs to his room.

They all knew what had happened. This woman.

This brave, stupid woman had protected his little girl.

He took her straight to his bedroom. No one made a sound as he did so. Placing her on his bed, he pushed some of her hair off her brow. Her blonde hair fanned out across his pillow, and he wanted her. His cock ached to be inside her, to claim her, to make her belong to him.

The past month had been sheer torture, but he could have lost her today. Both Jasmine and Bethany.

"I want this entire place on lockdown. No one leaves without my say-so. The wives have to come here as well."

"With the sweet-butts in residence?" Bear asked.

"Everyone. I want to know who put the hit on my house, and then I want to hurt the people that thought they could get away with shit like that." He craved blood and vengeance.

"There's going to be drama. A few cat fights. You know how Rave loves to fuck all the new chicks and his wife is never happy about finding out about it," Red said.

"I don't give a fuck. I've given you an instruction. Lock down immediately. I want info as soon as we have it."

"Boss, your girl is not happy. She's screaming. You're going to need to come down," Bear said. "She's out for the count."

Hawk stroked her cheek, knowing he was going to have his balls fucking handed to him the moment she woke up. She was going to be in pain, but there wasn't a lot he could do about that.

"I'll take care of her," he said. "Rest and don't hate me too much."

It didn't matter anymore. He wasn't about to let her escape from him now. Leaving his bedroom, he slid the door closed and went straight to the main room where he saw Bethany being passed from one person to another. Going straight up to one of the bitches that were holding her, he took his girl into his arms.

Bethany continued to cry and then slowly, calm. He knew Jasmine used his spare leather cuts to keep around her to try to show his little girl that she was safe with his scent around her.

Whatever worked.

She calmed down and rested her head against his chest.

He loved this little girl.

"You all heard what happened. Until I say otherwise, we're all on lockdown. I don't know who put that hit, and I didn't see any cuts or colors to say who the fuck it was. The license plate was a bust. It had been reported stolen three days before the hit. Either way, I will strike back." He just wouldn't be stupid enough to hit out at the first person he wanted to.

Stones's crew was always vying for territory, and he knew there was a recent order of guns from them. Hawk didn't see it being them, though. They had an agreement of sorts. They didn't step on his land, and he didn't fuck them up.

It was a simple agreement and one he'd stuck to. When you live this close to many different MCs and street gangs there had to be negotiations, as otherwise all-out war broke out and he wasn't above killing someone.

He'd done his fair share of killing to get the Satan's Rulers MC where it needed to be, and he'd be damned if anyone thought to take that from him or the woman that had entered his life.

Barking out his orders to his crew, he watched them all set off. First order of business, the old ladies needed to get here, and then their kids. Food had to be gathered, and once that was done, he made sure there was a present being organized for his woman.

Holding Bethany tight to him, he kissed the top of her head.

"Let's go and check on Jasmine," he said.

His nanny better be ready. He wasn't going to let her go, not now, not ever. He didn't know exactly what was going to happen between them, but he knew without a doubt she was destined to bounce on his cock.

For now, that was enough.

****

"You're going to be in pain," Hawk said.

Jasmine didn't even want to hear him right now. Her shoulder hurt, and she recalled the force with which the three men held her down.

"I want to go home," she said. "I quit."

The bed dipped, and she turned to see him sitting on the edge near her. His hand was on her hip, his fingers rubbing in a circular motion. She wasn't happy that her body liked that. Even with the dull pain in her shoulder, she responded to him. What the hell was wrong with her?

"You don't quit."

"At no point in the job description does it say dodge bullets. That wasn't what I was supposed to be doing. You put Bethany's life at risk."

"I'm going to find the people responsible and I'm going to deal with it."

"By shooting more people?"

"By taking care of business. It's what I do."

She glanced around the room. "Where is Bethany?"

"She's asleep in the nursery. When we're on lockdown we have one set up for all the kids to sleep. Being around other kids relaxes them."

She lifted her good arm and pressed a hand to her

face.

The pain was starting to get worse. "Why didn't he just knock me out to start with?"

"Because he needed to make sure you were fine and didn't have any adverse reaction. He's a good doctor," Hawk said.

She noticed his voice was soft as he spoke. "That makes sense, I guess. I still should have gone to the hospital."

"Regardless, you couldn't go. I won't have any cops sniffing around my club."

She let out a breath, very much aware of his caressing touch.

This was bad. She liked his touch a little too much.

"You need to stop that."

"Why?"

"Because it's not appropriate. I'm your nanny."

"While you're here, you're under my protection, Jasmine. That doesn't make you my nanny."

"What does it make me then?" she asked.

"It makes you mine. As far as the club is aware, they're not allowed to touch you because I've staked a claim on you."

"And if you hadn't done that?"

"You'd be fair game."

"I'm Bethany's nanny."

"To all of the guys here, you're fair game."

She didn't want to deal with this right now. Too much was going on.

"I'm upset," she said.

"I've got a present for you. I was going to give it to you in the morning, but I don't see the reason to wait anymore." He held something wrapped.

Lifting up in the bed until she sat up, she missed

his touch on her hip but didn't protest as he handed her the wrapped gift.

It looked like a book.

Turning it over, she saw a small slit that didn't have tape on, and slid her fingers beneath the wrapping. Opening it up with one hand, she was careful as she moved the other. She still had a lot of pain.

With the wrapping off, she turned it over and saw it was a book for a food mixer. Turning it over, she couldn't help but smile. "You bought me a food mixer?"

"It's set up downstairs. We don't know how long this lockdown's going to take. Whatever you need, just let me know and you can start baking and cooking up a storm. I saw you admiring it the other day while we were out shopping," he said.

"This is to stop me being pissed at you for holding me down?"

"It's for a lot of things, but if it'll make you not hate me, I'm all for it."

She stared at the book before looking at him. "You didn't have to get me anything."

"I didn't want you to hate me."

Jasmine had a feeling that he didn't allow himself to be open with a woman like this. Not for the first time she wondered about Bethany's mother. There were no pictures of her or any reminders of who she was.

Tucking some hair behind her ear, her stomach chose that moment to start to growl.

"Come on, there's some leftover takeout waiting for us."

"There is?" she asked. Her mouth watered.

Glancing down at her semi-nude state, she gave a wince. The pajamas she'd been wearing had a lot of blood all over them.

"Here, put these on." He handed her a pair of

shorts and a shirt.

"Whose room am I in?"

"Mine. You don't think I'd just put you anywhere, did you?" he asked.

Biting her lip, she glanced back at the bed. There were bloodstains on his sheet. "Don't worry about that. I'll get one of the whores to clean that up."

He took hold of her hand, and she had no choice but to go ahead and follow him.

"Do you really have to call them that?" she asked.

"That's what they are. Club whores. They service the club. Any member for whatever their need is."

"Yeah, but does it have to be so crude?" She wrinkled her nose, not liking the way he was talking about women.

He chuckled. "You've got a lot to learn about club life."

They passed the busy main room. Several of the men were being serviced by who she could imagine were the club whores. The women didn't seem to mind though. They looked totally happy to do their duty to their club.

One of the women was spread open with a cock in her mouth and another in her pussy. The scene before her was so shocking, and Jasmine was surprised by how aroused she became from just that glimpse of it.

Quickly averting her gaze and hating her confusion, she focused on the man in front of her who'd entered the kitchen.

He released her hand and then put his hands on the pink food mixer he'd purchased for it.

It looked so feminine within the dark, masculine kitchen.

"What do you think?" he asked.

She walked up to the mixer and smiled. "I can't

believe you bought it for me." She put a hand on the body and felt the cool metal. She loved it. As she stood there admiring it, she couldn't help but think of all the yummy cakes and cookies she intended to make. "It's awesome."

"So I'm forgiven?"

She pushed some more hair off her face. She was trying not to use her other hand as it had started to ache. "There's nothing to forgive. You did what you had to do, and besides, this is a pretty awesome gift."

"Good. Now, take a seat. I'll serve you."

She sat down at the table and couldn't help but admire his ass as he grabbed whatever he wanted out of the fridge.

In his domain, he was like a king, and in a way that was totally what he was, a king.

"What do they call you here? You're their leader."

"I'm their President. You'll hear them calling me 'Prez' or something like that."

"And that's a sign of respect?" she asked.

"Are you curious about the MC life, Jasmine?"

"No, not really. Maybe a little. I don't know. I just don't understand it. I would hate to be called a whore or to have to do that kind of thing."

"That's because you're not a club whore, babe. Far from it." He put several cartons on the table. "What would you like?"

"Anything."

She watched as he fixed her a plate. He handed her some chopsticks, and she waited as he served himself.

"You didn't have to wait."

"I wanted to." She offered him a smile, which he returned.

This was sort of surreal to her. She couldn't believe she was eating with her boss and not only that, she'd been shot.

"I'm a badass."

"What?"

"I've got a war wound. Look at me. I'm totally a badass." She couldn't help but smile, and he laughed right along with her.

Maybe this lockdown wouldn't be such a bad thing.

Chapter Five

The following day Hawk was not impressed to see Jasmine outside playing with Bethany. His little girl was on the ground with a few toys and Jasmine sat on the ground, leaning against a tree trunk for some shade.

"What are you doing?"

"We're basking in the sun rather than being cooped up in there. Other women and children are out." She pointed toward the parking lot where several of the old ladies stood. When he and Jasmine had gone to bed last night, there had been a fight between an old lady and a club whore.

The club whore had come out worse off with a broken nose. The old lady currently wasn't speaking to her old man. It was a bit of a disaster, but he was used to it. Mixing the two women never went well at all. There would always be some fallout. Especially if a club whore thought for a second she had a chance with one of the men at the club. There was always that rivalry that came into play.

His problem was the fact he didn't give a fuck about the other women. His only concern was for his two right here.

"I want you inside. It's not safe."

"Hawk, I've seen the guys all around the property. You've got three men at the front of the gate at all times, not to mention Prospects walking around the entire clubhouse. We're fine."

"Yeah, and at my place you had me. I'm as good as it's going to get for protection."

"Excellent, sit with us," she said. "That way we get the protection you want us to have and we also get to sit in the sun and bask in the heat. It's too hot inside."

"Fine." It *was* actually really safe. He was just

being cautious.

They were closer to finding out who'd ordered the hit. He'd reached out to Stones's crew, and they had told him it wasn't them. That the order they had for guns was for a transaction with someone else. As soon as he had all the details about the order of guns, as well as the information that two of his club boys had done during their recon, he'd figure out the best way to deal with the club involved. It was another MC; he knew that for a fact. He wouldn't even think of their name because by the time he was done with them, they weren't going to exist. No one would remember them.

Taking a seat on the grass, he stared at his little girl, who was shaking a rattle. Every now and again, she'd go to crawl and he'd hear Jasmine's soft laughter. Considering she was shot yesterday she was doing okay.

They'd gotten to talk last night, and he enjoyed it. It was weird for him to admit something like that, but he actually enjoyed just sitting with her, talking. No woman in his life had ever made him say that.

He often found them annoying, tedious, and only good for one thing.

Jasmine wasn't like that.

She moved, and he saw her wince.

"How's the shoulder?" he asked.

"It's fine. A little sore. My body is fine though. I guess I can't complain really. I had three men holding me down. Not many women could say that."

He burst out laughing.

"What?"

"Some of the women can top that."

"Oh, my God, I can't believe you just went there." She laughed. "You're going to have to watch your language around this one. Pretty soon, she'd be shocking you with her words."

"Yeah, I can imagine." He stroked Bethany's cheek. She looked up at him and smiled. She was growing up so fast.

"You really do love her?" she asked.

"She's my first kid. My only kid. Don't ask me to talk about her mother. I never will. Bethany deserved better than that traitor, got me?"

Jasmine held her hands up. "I won't say a word. When you look at her, I can see your love for her. It's nice."

"Regardless of where she came from, she's my flesh and blood. I'll do anything for her." He reached out and placed a hand near her shoulder. Jasmine jerked back just a touch.

"Sorry, I thought you were going to touch it."

"You protected my daughter yesterday rather than your own life. For that, I'll be permanently in your debt. I don't want anything to happen to her."

"Hawk, I know what it's like to lose a child. You're not in my debt. I hope if I ever have a child one day, then there'll be someone out there who'd protect my child just the same."

"Do you stay in touch with your husband?"

"No. I know he's moved on, and I accept that. To be honest, we probably shouldn't have even tried for a baby together."

"Why not?"

"We weren't in the best place. We'd spoken of divorce a couple of times, and then I found out I was pregnant. For a short time, it was fun. We had the baby to prepare for. To take care of. Our problems seemed to evaporate."

"Then you lost the baby."

"Then I lost the baby and nothing was the same again. I mean, in the beginning of our marriage, I loved him. Of course I did, but we both wanted different things. He didn't want to be a dad, you see. He didn't suggest I get rid of it or anything. He knew it was what I wanted, and we figured seeing as we were going to be parents, we may as well give our marriage another shot." She shrugged.

She didn't look sad about it ending.

"I've never been married."

"You haven't?"

"Never needed to. Women have come and gone all my life. I imagine it takes a special kind of woman to make a guy do something like that."

She chuckled. "Are you flirting with me?"

"Haven't you noticed?"

"I think I may have just figured you out."

He loved seeing her smile.

"Boss, we have something," Bear said, coming outside.

Jasmine seemed to wake up, their little bubble being interrupted. *Damn it.* He liked seeing her smile and relax, listening to her talk. It was so rare for him to have a few moments like this.

"I'll be there in a minute."

"Hawk?"

"I'll be there!" He growled out each word. Bethany started to whimper, and the moment truly was gone.

Jasmine moved behind his daughter, offering her some comfort.

Bear left, but the damage was done.

"I'll be back," Hawk said.

"Hawk," Jasmine said. "Don't get yourself hurt because of what happened. I'm fine with it. Well, I'm not, but I'm doing okay. I think I'm doing okay."

She didn't want him to be hurt.

"I won't get hurt. I promise." He nodded at her and at his little girl before heading inside.

Bear was waiting in his office with Red.

"Next time I'm out with her or my daughter, you fucking wait, do you understand?"

"You asked us to come and get you when there's been a development. There's been a development."

"I don't give a fuck. Don't ever interrupt me again."

"Is she your old lady, Prez?" Red asked.

He stared at his two men. He trusted the two of them with his life. They'd been by his side for the last decade, each one showing their loyalty to him and to the club. To claim an old lady added protection to her within the club.

The reason he didn't care about those women and kids in the parking lot was that he had this place so fucking secure they could do whatever they wanted.

When it came to Jasmine and Bethany, he couldn't fucking think straight.

"Yeah, she's my old lady."

There was no backing out now. Declaring her as such gave him a time limit. She'd have to know what he just declared.

"Make sure all the boys know who she is and that they have to give her respect no matter what. I want her protected."

"Got it, Boss," Red said. "Now, to business. We know who ordered the hit on you. It wasn't Stones's as we first thought."

Hawk moved toward the pictures that Red and Bear were looking over.

Things were about to get bloody.

****

Two days later

Bethany was down for the count for an afternoon nap. Jasmine's shoulder wasn't hurting her anymore. She was able to use it without much pain, so she made her way down to the kitchen. It had been nearly five days since she made anything. Takeout was starting to all taste the same, and the need to bake something was driving her crazy.

She wanted some fresh cookies, or maybe even a pie. It would all depend on how her arm was with lifting and carrying.

She passed several of the club whores, who avoided her.

Offering them a smile as she passed, she tried not to feel hurt when they completely ignored her.

It wasn't her problem why they did what they did.

Brushing off their rejection, she went straight into the kitchen to see it bare. Hawk had warned her that no one liked to cook or to clean it up. That as a space within the clubhouse it had been vacant and wasted for a long time.

She saw her machine, and when all this lockdown nonsense was over, she was totally taking it home and having some fun with it.

"Hello, baby." She laughed as she spoke to her new mixer. "We're going to have a lot of fun together."

She made sure it was plugged in and all set up as she made her way toward the fridge. Checking inside, she started to rummage around, looking at all the ingredients. There were a couple of rotting tomatoes, and she pulled some chicken out and saw it was green.

"Ew."

"Not in the best state, is it?"

She turned to see a brunette standing in the doorway.

"No. I was hoping to do something for dinner, but

it looks bad."

"They did go shopping. You're just going to have to go through the good and the bad. They don't believe in chucking anything away. Here, let me help you. I'm Renee," the brunette said.

"Jasmine."

"Ah, you're Hawk's old lady."

This made Jasmine pause and frown. "No, I'm not his old lady."

"It's okay. I'm not Bear's old lady either, but whenever something like this goes down, he seems to like bringing me along. It's exhausting, really."

Jasmine stared at the beautiful brunette, somewhat taken aback.

"I'm sorry, I don't quite follow."

"Bear and I went on one date together. It was great, but he decided this life and me wouldn't mix. I was fine with that. It was a fun date, no funny business. I was happy for us to not take things further, but he wasn't willing to let me move on, so that's why I'm here now and he's off doing whatever it is he's doing."

"I've not seen you around here for the past couple of days," Jasmine said. "Wait, hold on. So, he doesn't want you, but he doesn't want another man to have you?"

"Got it, honey. Yep, that's the way we roll. When I heard the club whores talking about you, I knew I had to come and see you, and to answer your other question, I've been protesting in his bedroom. He's not allowed in, and I don't come out." She shrugged. "I'm being a bitch, but he keeps interrupting all of my dates and I'm tired of it. I'm fighting back."

"I'm not Hawk's old lady."

"That's not what everyone is saying, and if the whores are talking, then it means it's true."

"They're gossiping. I'm his nanny."

Renee started to laugh. "Yeah, that's just so original. He's totally got a thing for you, honey. Hawk wants a piece of you."

Jasmine started to go through the fridge. She needed to clear her mind. There's no way that Hawk would consider her old lady material. She took care of his little girl. Glancing over at the baby monitor, she saw that Bethany was still sleeping.

Emptying out all of the bad food, she trashed it. With the fresh food, she piled it up onto the table, washed out the fridge with Renee's help, and then organized everything.

"You have an OCD thing going on?" Renee asked.

"No. I just ... I need to think."

"Hawk's a good guy."

"He's a biker. An MC person. I can't ... that's not happening."

"I'd be with Bear if he wasn't such an ass." Renee shrugged. "He's the one that gets to make all the decisions. News flash, I know my own mind. I can handle this life. What I can't handle is thinking of him with one of those skanks upstairs."

"Do you really need to call them that?" Jasmine asked. Whores and skanks, she felt bad for them.

"They'd fuck anything with a leather cut and a dick. Believe me, they're not worth it."

"I don't know, some of them seem nice."

"Since finding out that Hawk claimed you, they've done nothing but be bitchy about you. Believe me, they've got no intention of being nice to you."

"If it was true, why would they hate me?"

"Because Hawk is like a king in this place. All of them want a piece of him. Any woman that is his old lady, I mean, she's instantly protected. Taken care of.

Men know that they can look but they can't touch, and in truth, they shouldn't look at you either. It's a pretty important place to be."

As she stared down at the large package of chicken breasts, her mind whirled with what this could mean.

"You're worried."

"I'm only his nanny. The company I work for has a clause, and I don't want to lose my position and place there. I don't … we met at the grocery store before I even knew that he was the person I would be working for. Then this." She pointed at her shoulder. "Now I can't make sense of anything."

"Maybe it's nothing to make sense of. It happened."

"I don't want to lose my job."

"If I was you, I'd talk to him. But then, what do I know? Bear doesn't even give me a chance to talk anymore. If I don't do as he says, he just puts me over his shoulder and carries me to where he needs to be."

Jasmine saw the smile on the woman's face. "You like that?"

"A little bit. It's kind of cool to watch him. He has something about him that makes it impossible for me to stay mad at him for anything longer than a few hours. The things we do for men. Are you wanting to cook them all dinner?"

"Yeah, or us. I don't know. Would it be silly to make, like, a big casserole or something like that?"

"I don't think so. You may even get some of the guys to fall in love with you. Most of them don't end up going home. Too much trouble with the old lady, if you know what I mean."

She had a feeling she did but didn't comment.

With Renee's help, she got all of the ingredients

prepped and ready. Using several large casserole pots, she assembled six pots and made a note to cook up some biscuits or something to put on the side so everyone had plenty.

She left Renee to put everything in the oven as Bethany woke up. It was a struggle to take care of Bethany with a wound in her shoulder but not impossible. Once she brought the little girl downstairs, she saw Renee was already making the crust for the pecan pie she intended to make.

"She's a little angel," Renee said.

Jasmine put her in the high chair. "She's so wonderful to take care of."

"I can't believe he's got a kid. It's kind of funny though that he got a girl. It's like karma has come to bite him in the ass." Renee laughed. "I was thinking you and I could hang out sometime. Just the two of us. Away from the club."

"After the lockdown?"

"Yeah. You and me, a possible spa day or a girls' night. What do you think?"

"You're not going to get her into trouble," Hawk said.

She hadn't even heard him return.

Bethany gave a squeal as he lifted her up, and Jasmine watched his daughter snuggle in against him. It wasn't that long ago she was screaming to get away.

Pushing some hair out of her eyes, Jasmine saw he was looking a little tired.

"Your girl needs some fun. Are you going to ink that?" Renee asked.

"Ink what?"

"Your scar. I know a great place that will give you killer ink."

She looked at her bandaged shoulder and gave a

little shrug. "I hadn't really thought that far ahead, you know." Could she have a tattoo? "I'm scared of needles." She hated them and would do everything to avoid them.

Renee chuckled. "Hawk's got plenty of tattoos. He can talk you through it."

She stared at Hawk. "We need to talk."

"That sounds serious," Bear said.

Bear walked into the kitchen, pulling Renee into a hug. "How are you doing, babe?"

"I'm not talking to you."

"You just did."

"You mind watching Bethany for me?" Hawk asked. "It looks like I'm about to get a piece of her mind."

Chapter Six

It was only a matter of time before Jasmine found out the truth. Hawk watched as she paced the length of his bedroom. She sucked her bottom lip in. He knew what she wanted to talk about.

The brothers had warned him there had been a lot of talk. He'd have stayed at the clubhouse today, but he wanted to check out the MC that thought they could take him out. They were ten miles out of town, in a shitty, run-down old garage. They had a metal fence, and dogs that they kept on fucking leashes. Women came and went. They looked a lot better entering the MC than they did leaving it.

He'd paid a couple of the women for information.

The setup looked sloppy, but he wasn't willing to risk his men without knowing everything first. This was one of the reasons he was damn good at what he did. He only took the necessary risks and rarely did any of his men suffer.

Being out today meant Jasmine was alone with all the potential rumors.

"I'm not your old lady," she said, stopping in front of him.

He didn't say a word, watching her as she ran fingers through her hair.

"Why do they think I'm your old lady? Renee told me that some of the other … women hate me because you've made this declaration of some kind. I don't understand it."

"It's simple. You're my old lady."

"No, Hawk. I'm your nanny. That's it."

"It's more than that." He wasn't going to sit and listen to her try to make out that there was nothing going on between them.

The first day they met, he felt something.

If it hadn't been for Bethany or the fact he was interviewing for a nanny, he'd have taken her out on a date or at least done something. Instead, what he'd done was let her go. When she entered his clubhouse, he'd known his chance was over with. The company he'd been using had told him their views on relationships between clients.

Fucking the nanny wasn't going to be an option.

He'd kept his distance.

It had only been a month, but that was more than enough time for him to know what he wanted and who he wanted.

He stood up.

Jasmine took a step back.

With each step he took, she moved back until she hit the wall.

Slamming his hands against the wall, he saw her jump.

"What are you doing?"

He saw her eyes dilate.

He glanced down her body, and the shirt she wore was like a second skin over her tits, her hard nipples pressing against the front.

"You feel this, Jasmine. I won't listen to you say otherwise. I know you do. I can see that you do." He cupped her cheek, tilting her head back.

"I love my job. I don't want to lose it."

"They won't find out. Not right now."

"They do checks, Hawk. I love my job."

"Your job right now is to take care of Bethany and me."

"I'm not *your* nanny."

He saw her fighting this. "Okay, we'll play this your way for a time, but I will warn you, I don't play fair."

Before she could say anything else, he slammed his lips down on hers, silencing her.

She released a moan. Her hands gripped his hips, and she was running them up his chest.

Cupping her hip, he caressed down to her thigh, lifting it high on his hip so that he could rock his cock against her core.

She gasped, and he plundered into her mouth, tasting her.

Breaking from her lips, he kissed down her neck, sucking on her tender flesh. She was so fucking tasty. His cock was rock-hard. He wanted inside her, fucking her hard. Instead, he held off, waiting, listening, and then he heard that groan, the one that told him she was hungry and desperate for more.

"Please."

That was all he was waiting for.

Pulling away, he gave her a smile.

"Then maybe you should make a decision as to whether you want to be my old lady or not."

He let her go, and without waiting for her to say anything else, he followed the sound of Bethany's cries.

Humming to himself, he didn't linger. Picking up his baby girl, he carried her outside into the warm, fresh air.

She giggled while still holding the rattle.

Putting her down on the ground beneath a tree, he sat down and watched as she crawled around. Every now and then, she'd stop and push her fist into her mouth, looking so cute as she did.

"Your girl's in trouble," Bear said, dropping down beside him.

"Why?"

"Renee likes her and is trying to convince her to

go out. The last time Renee went out, she ended up hanging out of my truck because she wouldn't stay the fuck inside it."

"When are you going to pull your head out of your ass and claim her?"

"Probably never," Bear said. "She's too good for me."

"Bullshit. You've always pushed her away. I don't get it."

"Simple. I want her to have whatever she wants. A life filled with love and no heartache. This life, it eats women like Renee. I couldn't stand to hurt her."

"Pussy."

"Fuck you."

"Have you ever thought that she's the kind of girl you don't hurt? That you're *not* going to hurt her. What do I know? I buried the mother of my kid after I killed her, so I'm not one to talk."

"Your girl know that you put the old lady patch on her?" Bear asked.

"She knows."

"She happy about it?"

"Fuck no, she's not. I'm not going to take it away though. Jasmine's mine." He laughed. "Jasmine, mine, get it. She's mine."

"You're getting way too fucking old."

"Fuck off." He stopped Bethany from going onto the path and placed her back on the grass.

"What are you going to do about that then, Boss? Your woman didn't exactly look thrilled at the idea of belonging to you."

"She'll get used to it."

"You think you're acting too quickly?"

"Have you gotten a pussy, Bear? I swear you're starting to sound like a fucking girl."

Bear burst out laughing. "Just got your back, Prez. I know what happened the last time with a woman. Last thing I'd want is for you to get hurt."

"That's not going to happen. Jasmine's different."

"When do you want to do this hit?" Bear asked, changing the conversation.

"When we know more. We know they're armed, we just don't know how much."

"Do you want to send a guy in undercover?"

"No. I don't want this playing out that long. We'll keep on checking them out. Wait for some mistakes to shine through and then we'll handle them." He had no doubt that within a few weeks he'd know everything there was to know.

"I don't suppose you wish to be bait?"

He looked at Bear.

"To speed this shit along. You look vulnerable, unprotected. They take you out or they assume they take you out?"

"It won't work," Hawk said.

"Why?"

"The hit on my house was totally random. If they intended to kill, they'd have come inside. This was a warning to us. Believe me, I got it loud and clear." Just thinking about that morning and how fucking terrified he'd been for Bethany and Jasmine, filled him with rage. "I don't intend to be anyone's bait. We'll get them, Bear. Patience is all we need. They're going to fuck up."

If it wasn't for the hit on the house he'd have already attempted to take them out. They had their own weapons to fight back.

Hawk was being cautious.

A year ago, he'd have done that hit without a second thought. With a daughter and now a woman in his life, he wasn't going to make that mistake again.

Renee made her way outside, and Bear stood just a little taller.

"Dinner's nearly ready," she said.

"On a scale of one to ten, how pissed is she right now?"

"She's quite up there. It looks like you've got your work cut out for you in making amends there, biker boy." Renee smiled at him before turning her weary gaze on Bear.

These two really needed to fuck and make a decision. Or should he say, Bear needed to.

"Dinner's ready," she said again.

She didn't wait around. Turning on her heel, she walked back to the clubhouse. It was the first time Hawk had seen her during this lockdown.

"You're drooling," he said.

"That ass."

"You really need to stop being an asshole and claim that woman."

"She's not—"

"I get it, right for the club. You ever thought she's totally right for you? None of the old ladies are right for the club. In some way we're going to ruin them, but it's what you feel that makes the difference." He picked up Bethany and stared at his friend and VP.

"Now who has the pussy?" Bear asked, smirking.

"I've got the pair of balls. You see, I laid claim to my woman. You're just panting after yours like a little puppy dog." He saw Bear's glare, but he didn't linger to see what his friend would say.

Taking his daughter inside, he took a moment to watch Jasmine as she served everyone some food.

This place would do wonders for her. She liked to be needed, and right now she was needed a whole hell of a lot.

****

Lying in bed, Jasmine tried to focus on the murder mystery book she'd found in the top drawer of his nightstand. She loved to read, mostly romance, but every now and then she delved into a book that was a little different from her usual style.

Bethany was already down for bed and in recent days had been sleeping throughout the night.

The first thing she'd done when Hawk hired her was to develop a routine with Bethany that included spaced-out naps and times for play and stimulation with activities that meant by the time night came, she was exhausted.

If he was downstairs, did that mean one of the women that liked to fuck random men was dealing with him?

The thought of him sitting there as one of the women took care of his needs, filled her with a jealousy she didn't want to think about.

"Let him." She gritted her teeth, hating the feeling that was riding up inside her at the thought of him being with another woman. Of another woman sucking on his cock or riding him to completion.

Was he the kind of man that held a woman down and fucked her?

All the dirty thoughts running through her head were *not* helping.

Just as she was about to throw the book at the damn door, it opened and Hawk walked in. He didn't look like he'd been with another woman. He closed the door behind him.

He'd already told her before she walked upstairs that he'd be joining her tonight in this bed.

She didn't exactly know what that meant, but she was intrigued. Was he just going to snuggle in? Were they going to fool around? Have sex?

Fool around?

How old are you?

"Hello," she said.

"Interesting book."

She smiled. "Yes."

"What part are you at?"

"Erm, part?"

"Yeah."

"You've read it?"

"I do read."

"Of course you do."

"I'm at the start."

He chuckled.

"I am reading it."

"Sure you are."

She ignored him, watching as he removed his leather cut. The shirt he wore clung to his muscular arms. He'd not let himself go at forty-five years old. Every single inch of him was pure, hard steel. Whoever thought to take a hit out on him were idiots as far as she was concerned. There's no way he'd ever let that kind of thing stand.

"Did you have fun downstairs?" she asked. She gritted her teeth after she spoke since she didn't want to draw attention to the fact she was a little pissed at him for being downstairs with those other women.

She didn't want to call them whores or skanks as that just felt so rude.

"Fun?"

"You know? Partying and stuff."

He smirked as he pulled his shirt off, showing all of his ink. Biting her lip, she tried to ignore her own arousal at seeing him get naked.

Hawk stood at the edge of the bed, hands on hips,

smiling down at her.

"You want to tell me what's going on?"

"I just … you took your time. You must have been … you know, busy." She lifted up the book so she wasn't tempted to stare at his perfect body anymore.

He moved and suddenly the book was out of her hands and he pulled her from the bed. She didn't fight him as she stared into his green eyes. There wasn't anything about him that she didn't find attractive. She loved how shockingly green his eyes were, the fact he had grey hair at his temples, and even all of his ink.

"You jealous, baby?" he asked.

"No. Of course not." She scoffed at the mere idea of it, feeling like such a fucking liar as she spoke.

He smiled. "So, you don't have a problem with the thought of another woman touching me." He placed her hand on his chest. "Or another woman getting me hard." He moved her hand to his dick.

He wasn't small by any means.

Gripping his length, she knew he was going to hurt her when he entered her. She hoped he fit.

Licking her dry lips, she was mesmerized by his voice.

"Do you like the idea of another woman stripping me naked? Taking my cock in her mouth? Sucking it to the back of her throat so she gags on it?"

"Stop it," she said.

He banded an arm around her waist and pulled her in close, trapping her hand between their bodies. She couldn't look away from him though.

"I'm a lot of things, Jasmine. I've done a lot of shit to protect me and mine. But I can promise you, I'll never, ever step out on you. No other woman will suck my cock or ride my dick. The only mouth, pussy, and ass I'm going to know is yours." His other hand cupped her cheek. He ran a thumb ran across her bottom lip and slid it inside. "Fuck me, baby, I'm going to love every second of this."

She held onto his cock, rubbing him.

This was so wrong.

She could lose her job.

It had been so long since she'd felt a man's touch.

As he claimed her lips, she gave in to this need curling inside her. She didn't want to fight him or these feelings anymore.

It had only been a day, not even a full twenty-four hours, but from what Renee had told her about those other women, she wasn't happy with him being alone with them. She didn't want him to find his pleasure there, but to come to her.

He broke the kiss, and she whimpered, not wanting him to stop. His lips were at her ear, and she moaned.

"I'm going to stop now, but remember, I won't unless you tell me otherwise." He pressed a kiss to her head and took a step back.

Staring at him, she couldn't stop panting.

Her pussy was on fire and her nipples so hard.

"What's it going to be, Jasmine?"

She loved her job so much.

They don't have to know.

This was so wrong.

She wasn't a naughty girl.

Never had been.

All of her life, she'd followed the rules. Done everything by the book.

Hawk was everything that went against the book. He didn't follow any rules.

It was all his own way or no way.

Biting her lip, she stared down the length of his

body. Even in a pair of jeans, she saw the ridge of his dick. How hard he was pressing against the front of his jeans. It was too much temptation.

Staring into his eyes, she gripped the edge of her shirt, ignoring the bite of pain in her shoulder as she lifted it over her head and put it to the floor. Wriggling out of his boxer briefs, she stood before him naked.

He was the first man to see her completely naked in a very long time.

She was so nervous.

This was incredibly wild for her.

Stepping close to him, she placed a hand on his stomach.

"This doesn't mean I'm your old lady," she said.

He gripped her hips before running his hands up and down her back.

"You want to be my whore for the night?"

She wrinkled her nose. "No, I want to belong to you. I just … I'm scared of what it all means. I want this with you, Hawk. I'm just don't want you to throw me away when you realize I'm no good at this."

"There's no way you're not good at this. I'm ready to fucking explode now," he said. He gripped her ass and thrust his cock against her stomach. "You feel that. There's no way that anyone who makes me that hard is going to be bad at it."

She wanted to believe him.

"Are you sure about this? Once I start, there's no backing down."

"I don't want you to back down." She was ready for this. "I'm all yours, Hawk. Do whatever you want with me."

To Jasmine, that sounded so incredibly dirty, and she was ready. So ready.

Chapter Seven

Jasmine was so fucking curvy and ripe, her tits so large they filled his hands and spilled over. She had a curved-in waist, flared hips, and thick thighs that were designed to have a man fuck her hard.

Gripping her ass cheeks, he spread them open before releasing them and giving them a little slap.

She let out a gasp.

"Trust me," he said.

"I do."

Running his hands up to her face, he cupped her cheeks and took the kiss he couldn't seem to get enough of.

There was no way he was going to be able to stop once he got started. He fucking craved her more than anything else in the world.

No woman had ever made him feel like this. So possessed with need that he couldn't think straight.

He couldn't believe that she thought he was downstairs being fucked by one of the club whores. Since meeting her, he'd not played with any of them. It's why he knew they were going to be pissed with Jasmine because he'd made a claim and now they all knew they didn't have a chance with him.

They never would have a chance with him.

Jasmine was all he wanted and all he needed. She thought she didn't have what it took to satisfy him. He was going to prove her wrong. She was everything as far as he was concerned.

She attacked his belt, pulling it out of the loops as he walked her backward until she hit the wall.

Kissing down to her neck, he sucked on her pulse before trailing his lips down her body. His jeans were partly open, and as he took her nipple into his mouth and sucked on the bud, he wriggled them off.

They fell to the floor with a thud. Kicking them aside, he licked across her chest, circling the other bud. Moving his hands down her body, he cupped between her thighs, finding her wet cunt.

The lips of her pussy were covered in small curls that were damp from her arousal. Sliding a finger between her slit, he pushed inside.

She was so tight, and she moaned.

As far as he was concerned, she wasn't wet enough for him. Dropping to his knees before her, he lifted up her thigh and stared at her slit. Her clit was already swollen, and her cunt looked so tight.

He grabbed a chair and pulled it toward them. "Keep your foot on there."

"What are you doing?"

"I'm looking at what is mine."

He stared between her thighs at the same time he placed a finger on her slit. Moving down, he slid it inside her, watching her pussy.

She tightened around him and released a moan, so he added a second digit, stretching her.

Leaning forward, he sucked on her clit, and the cries coming from her were so damn hot.

His cock stood out, and he wrapped his fingers around the length, rubbing in the pre-cum that was already spilling out of the tip.

Up and down, he worked his length.

She was so damn tight around his two fingers he was surprised he even fit at all.

Adding a third finger, he flicked his tongue back and forth, arousing her even more.

He felt her release building, but he wasn't done with her yet. He didn't want her to come so quickly.

Pulling his fingers from her pussy, he stood up.

Staring into her eyes, he sucked his digits clean.

He saw her gaze widen.

"You're a dirty girl, aren't you?" he asked. "Has any man ever made you come so hard?"

"Please," she said.

He moved her this time to the bed. "Lie down. Spread those legs."

She moved to the center of the bed, opening her thighs wide. Staring at her body, he saw her pussy open, slick, and ready.

"Don't worry, baby. I'll treat you like a lady out there, but in here, I don't want you to be prim and proper. I want you to be dirty, to be horny, and to be begging for what you want."

Her cheeks were on fire.

"What do you want?" he asked.

"I want you."

"No, tell me exactly what you want."

She licked her lips. She took several deep breaths.

"I want your cock inside me. I want you to fuck me and then make me suck you off. Tasting us both."

He wrapped his fingers around his dick, running his hand up and down the length. Crawling on the bed, he straddled her waist. Gripping the back of her neck, he smiled. "Then have a taste now."

She didn't hesitate. She leaned forward, taking his cock into her mouth, moaning as her tongue flicked across his pre-cum.

He didn't know how he got so lucky, but as she took his cock to the back of her throat and gagged on it just a little before pulling up, he knew he'd scored with this woman. She was so fucking hot as he pumped his hips.

She didn't touch his cock.

Hawk held his dick, feeling her lips brush his

fingers as she sucked on him.

He was so close to coming, but he held himself back, counting to ten in his mind to have some kind of control.

When he knew he couldn't take anymore, he pulled out of her mouth, and she pouted.

"When we're here together, I want *this* woman," he said, cupping her face, slamming his lips down on hers.

She moaned.

Moving between her thighs, he slid his cock against her pussy, pressing against her clit. Thrusting back and forth, he heard her cry out, and he moved down, poised at her entrance. He stopped the kiss so that he could stare into her eyes.

With her gaze on him, he started to push inside her. Inch by inch, he stretched her tight cunt.

She gasped, and he slammed to the hilt inside her, feeling her warm pussy squeeze him.

"Oh, fuck, Jasmine. I'm never going to want to leave." He pulled out only to slam inside her. He did this several times as she wrapped her legs around his waist.

It would be so easy for him to come, to flood her pussy with his spunk.

He pulled out and lifted her up. Sliding his tongue across her pussy, he sucked on her clit.

She cried his name, the sound echoing around the room, and he fucking loved it.

That's all he wanted to hear coming from her lips as he fucked her harder than he'd ever taken a woman.

She panted his name, and as she came, he licked her cream, relishing the taste of her sweetness.

Pushing his cock inside her, he started to fuck her, holding her hands above her head.

"I'm not going to last for this one, baby. Next

time though, we'll explore that dirty side of yours."

He pushed inside her, fucking her. Looking down at where they were joined, he watched his cock, slick with her cream as he pounded away.

"Look at us, baby. Look at my cock inside you. So fucking good. You're so perfect." Driving inside her, he felt the first stirrings of his orgasm as it started to build.

He didn't stop, fucking her to his release, which he thrust in deep, flooding her pussy.

Hawk didn't give a flying fuck that he'd not worn a condom or what it could mean.

All that he cared about was how good she felt wrapped around his length.

Jasmine was perfect to him.

So beautiful.

All his.

He wanted to own and to possess every inch of her, and he had no intention of ever letting her go.

****

Jasmine stared up at the stars. She had on a robe to hide the nightshirt she'd thrown on. Everything had changed tonight.

After Hawk had come inside her, someone banged on the door, demanding his attention. She hated having to share him in that moment.

For a short time, it was like a blanket had covered them and it didn't matter what was said or done. His touch had awakened something inside her. Something she'd been hiding for so long, even when she was married.

Sex was … boring.

She'd always found it a chore.

Closing off that need that curled inside her when her ex would screw her, she'd lie there, make all the right noises and pretend that he was the best man on earth. That's what women did, right? They pretended everything was fine. It was part of the reason they were struggling as a couple. She couldn't keep faking it.

The needs that were building inside her wouldn't disappear.

She couldn't make them close off or turn them away. She'd wanted and craved the fire, the passion, and the dirty talk that Hawk had given her a glimpse of.

It was like she'd finally found someone who got her, and she'd been unable to turn it off. The way he'd presented his cock to her mouth. The way his pre-cum slid across her tongue. There hadn't been enough to taste him, and she'd wanted to be dirty so badly.

Staring up at the stars, she felt tears in her eyes.

For so long she'd thought she was wrong.

That she'd fucked up.

That she wanted stuff that no normal woman wanted.

What if the lie was everything she believed she was supposed to have?

This wasn't supposed to be the way her life went.

"I've been looking for you," Hawk said, drawing her attention.

Wiping the tears that had fallen onto her cheeks, she turned to look at him. "Don't worry. I've still listening for Bethany. I just needed some fresh air. Is everything okay?"

"Yeah, everything is fine." He moved up to the bench, his hands going to her knees and sliding down beneath the robe and her nightshirt. His fingers were so close to her pussy. "What's wrong?"

"It's nothing."

"Don't tell me that. Don't hide this shit from me, Jasmine. I'm not going back to you just being my nanny.

I know too much. You've shown me something, and I'm not going to let you get away with that."

"It's stupid."

"Nothing that you could ever want is stupid."

"I'm not this person."

"What person is that?" he asked.

She glanced around the back of the clubhouse and leaned close, whispering. "The kind of girl that gags on your cock or gets turned on by your talk. I'm not her." She moaned as his fingers stopped teasing and touched her pussy while she sat there on the bench. To anyone looking, it would seem that he was touching her legs, nothing more.

With both of his hands on her pussy, he spread her lips and his fingers teased her. "You feel that? It's you and me together. My cum is dripping from your pussy, making you so wet." He pressed fingers inside her, she didn't know how many. "You think what I saw upstairs was wrong? I think it was the most beautiful thing I've ever witnessed." He leaned in close so that his lips were at her neck, near her ear. "I love that no one knows the real you. That they don't even have a clue how wet you are right now and want to feel my cock deep inside you. I love that you have this part of you, Jasmine. A part that has been unexplored for so long." He pulled his fingers from her pussy, and he placed two fingers at her lips. "Taste us."

She opened her mouth, and he slid them up.

Jasmine tasted their combined release and gave a moan. Once his fingers were clean, he sank them into her hair, and tilted her head back to lay claim to her lips. His tongue traced across her mouth, and she opened up.

He plunged inside, and she moved to the edge of the bench, spreading her legs wide. He stepped between them.

His cock was already rock-hard.

They were out in the open. Anyone could see them.

She didn't care, as he opened the robe and lifted up her shirt.

"Take my cock out," he said, breaking the kiss.

Without dropping her gaze, she reached out to his pants, unbuttoning them, sliding down the zipper, and reaching in to take his cock.

He'd not put on any boxer briefs, so she didn't have to fight with the elastic that kept them up.

His jeans fell down; she heard them as the belt clattered against the ground.

"Touch me."

She wrapped her fingers around his dick, working the length up and down.

"You think I've got a problem with what you need? I fucking love it, baby, and believe me when I say we're going to explore this."

He pushed her hand away, and he broke their gazes. It didn't last for long as he ran the tip of his cock between her slit.

Looking down, even in the small outdoor light, she saw enough that she moaned. How could she not? It looked sexy as hell. Her pussy was so wet, and this time when Hawk thrust inside her, he did so with ease.

She was so wet and ready for him.

He pushed her down across the bench, lifting up the nightshirt to expose her tits.

He cupped the two mounds, and she watched him as he flicked his tongue across each nipple. The sensation created an answering pull between her thighs.

She wanted him.

Hawk didn't make her wait for long.

He pulled out of her only to slam back inside.

The bench wasn't the most comfortable place to be to get fucked, but she didn't want to move. When she made to wrap her legs around him, he stopped her, keeping her feet to the bench so that it opened her up.

He stood up so that he was no longer pinning her to the bench.

"I want to watch you touch your pussy," he said.

At first, she hesitated.

"No. I don't want you to listen for her. I want you to touch yourself. I want to see you lose control. Let me feel you as you come all over my cock. Give this to me, baby."

She slid a hand between them and touched her pussy. The first stroke against her clit made her cry out. She was so hungry for more. She didn't want to stop.

Gliding down, she felt the hard ridge of his cock as he fucked her. Touching him, she felt how wet he was, how wet she was. She'd never been like this, not ever.

Stroking her clit, she stared up at him, and couldn't believe she was outside in the middle of the night, where anyone could find them, fucking her boss.

Hawk was her boss.

The scary biker guy with the cute daughter.

Pushing those thoughts aside, she focused on him.

There was no going back after this.

She'd already crossed that line, and it made her wonder for a split second if this was what the other women went through at the agency. The attraction to an employer that just made them cross that line. She was in no way different now.

"Come for me, Jasmine. Come."

She worked her clit, feeling her arousal build until she came, calling out his name as she tightened around his cock.

He held her hips and fucked her harder, if that

was even possible. The bench didn't move even as he drove within her, taking her to a new height of arousal. Nothing made sense to her in that moment.

Hawk clouded everything, and as she felt him slam inside her one final time and his cum spill deep within her, she didn't want this to stop.

He didn't pull out of her immediately. He stayed still within her, and she stared up at him, in a bit of shock that she'd done this again.

She placed her hands over his and released a sigh.

"You're incredible."

"You're not too bad yourself."

They both looked toward the edge of the clubhouse as they heard laughter.

Hawk pulled out of her, and helped her pull on the robe.

Within seconds, they both didn't look like they'd fucked each other's brains out, and as Bear and another woman rounded the corner, Jasmine stared at the ground.

"Wonderful night," Hawk said.

"I better head inside," she said.

Without waiting for a response, she rushed inside the clubhouse, hoping no one saw through the robe or could see his cum sliding down her thigh.

Chapter Eight

Bethany had woken up once during the night and Hawk had made Jasmine stay in bed as he attended to his little girl.

Staring at the monitor, he saw Bethany was still fast asleep, and his woman was as well. She wore the shirt he'd given her last night. The blanket was thrown across her stomach. The shirt had ridden up, showing off her pretty pussy, and he wanted inside her again.

His cock hardened at the memory of her tightness wrapped around him.

He didn't think for a second he'd ever stop wanting her. In fact, he knew it.

She rolled over, and her eyes opened.

Smiling down at her, he waited for everything they'd done last night to come back to her. When it did, she lifted the blanket up to her face, glancing at him over the top. "That wasn't a dream, was it?"

"Not even close." He laughed. Tugging on the blanket, he refused to let her hide.

"I'm going to lose my job."

"You're not, and even if they don't hire you again, I've got a permanent place here for you. Bethany adores you, and I think you're okay."

She burst out laughing. "Okay?"

"A little more than okay, but I'm not about to get you thinking you can walk all over me." He cupped her pussy and she gasped, moaning.

As he slid a finger in deep, Jasmine spread her legs wide, giving him better access.

"Wait, wait. Hold on. I have a few conditions," she said.

He sighed. "Can you tell me them while I finger this perfect pussy?"

"No. I need you to focus on me."

"I am focusing on you and this tight cunt."

"Please. Just for me."

"Fine, fine. I'm listening." He withdrew his finger, but didn't stop touching her. Keeping his hand over her pussy, he waited. "I can hear everything you're saying."

"You're going to make this so difficult for me."

"Yep."

She giggled. "Fine. I don't want you screwing anyone else."

"Already done."

"No, I mean it. Those other women can't have anything to do with you. If you want your needs attended to then you've got to come to me."

"Already there, babe. 'Other women'?"

"The women that are part of this club."

"What women?" he asked, knowing exactly who she was talking about.

"I'm not going to call them what you and your men do. That's not right."

"It's what they are."

"It doesn't make it right. I'm not going to say it."

"I won't fuck any of the whores. My cock is for you and you only."

"Good." She pressed a kiss to his lips, which he found utterly sweet.

"Another condition?"

"Yes. This one isn't such a big one, but you might not like it."

"Let's hear it then."

"If this doesn't work out between us and the agency discovers it, could you help me find another job? This one is really serious. I want to be able to support myself, and if I can't work as a nanny I'm going to need help."

He placed a finger against her lips. She looked so damn scared and worried. He hated that look.

"I'll help you find and do anything. You don't even need to worry about that stuff. I'm here." He had no intention of ever letting her go.

She was so good with Bethany, and he loved her riding his cock.

"Is that all?" he asked.

"That's all."

"Good, now can I deal with my morning wood?"

"Oh, my, how can you … ohh, that feels so good."

He pushed two fingers inside her, stroking his thumb back and forth over her clit.

She pushed her pelvis up against his hand and whimpered as he kept on teasing her. Her cunt tightened around him, sucking on his digits as he worked her body.

Pulling his fingers from her pussy, he moved down the bed, grabbing her hips and turning her so that she was on her knees. He got off the bed and stared down at her perfect. heart-shaped ass.

Running his hands all over, he spread the cheeks wide, staring at the pretty anus and the soaking wet slit.

His cock was already rock-hard with copious amounts of pre-cum spilling from the tip. He wrapped his fingers around the length. With his other hand, he teased her pussy, drawing some of her cream back to stroke across her anus. She let out a little gasp, and he couldn't resist smiling.

"You ever had a fat cock here?" he asked.

"No."

"I'll show you just how good it can be."

"I doubt it can be good."

"You won't know what you've been missing all

this time. Don't worry, I'll get you nice and prepared." Rubbing his slick fingers across her ass, he watched her tense up at first. He teased across her anus, pressing against that puckered hole.

The muscles kept him out at first.

He wasn't a man to be denied.

Pushing past that tight ring of muscles, he filled her ass, listening to her moans as he pumped in and out of her.

Stepping forward, he placed the tip of his dick at her entrance and slowly filled her pussy as he worked a second finger inside her ass.

"Play with your pussy, baby. I want to feel you come."

She began to stroke, and with his dick balls deep within her, he played with her ass, getting her accustomed to the feel of him.

With two fingers inside her, he was able to stretch her. Each thrust inside, she'd tense up, and he'd wait for her to relax before doing the same thing again. With his hand on the base of her back, he held her still as he pulled his cock out of her, and saw her cum soaking his dick.

Slamming back in, he closed his eyes, enjoying the pleasure of her squeezing him.

Rocking back and forth within her, he couldn't resist watching her once again. Pumping his cock and fingers within her pussy and ass, he worked her until she was gasping.

When she finally came, shouting his name, he gripped her hip, slamming deep within her one final time and filling her with his cum.

It was the best way of waking up in the morning. Pressing a kiss to her ass, he pulled out of her, seeing his cum spill from the lips of her pussy.

He couldn't resist cupping his creamy mixture and pushing it back inside her.

"You're not begging me to wear a condom," he said.

"You don't need to. I'm on the pill. I'm clean."

"I'm clean as well, babe." He didn't like that she was on the pill.

Hawk didn't like what he was thinking either.

"Come on. Let's take a shower, and then I've got to handle church." He took her hand, leading her into the en-suite bathroom. They wouldn't have much longer before Bethany woke up.

"I could get used to this," she said. Her head tilted back, the spray hitting her face.

Her blonde locks looked darker as the water cascaded over her.

Grabbing the soap, he washed his hands, and then used them to soap her body. He took his time, caressing her skin, going all over, not leaving a part of her untouched, getting her nice and clean.

Hawk couldn't think of the best part of her body. He loved every single inch of her. He adored her ass, and when he was pounding that little asshole, he'd be in heaven. Her pussy was so tight and he loved being inside her. He knew from the moment he met her, once would never be enough. Then you had her tits. So big and juicy, he could suck on them for days.

Cupping the mounds now, he held them up to the water before giving them another taste.

So perfect.

"Please, Hawk," she said.

"You want to come again?"

"Yes, please. Yes."

"Tell me to make you come."

"Please, Hawk, make me come."

He pressed her against the cold tile, forcing her to lift a leg up so that he had easier access to do all the wicked things that he wanted to do to her.

Sliding his hand up between her thighs, he cupped her already filled pussy. Drawing his fingers out, he slid them across her clit. Her moans filled the bathroom. He loved the sounds she made. Pushing two fingers inside her, he took one of her nipples into his mouth, sucking on it. Moving across to her other nipple, he lathered that with the same kind of attention before kissing down her body. When he was on his knees before her, he stared at her pussy. "This all has to come off." He pulled his fingers from her pussy, teasing through the strands of hair.

"What?"

"I want you bare. Will you let me do that to you, baby?"

He stared up at her, waiting.

She bit her lip, looking so nervous.

"I'll do a good job."

"O-okay."

He pressed a kiss to her leg and grabbed the soap and his razor. He'd put a fresh blade into his razor, and he soaped up the fine hairs of her pussy before running the blade across her tender flesh. She tensed the moment he touched her skin, but after the second stroke, he watched as she relaxed against his touch.

Hawk wasn't in a rush, and with the final sweep, she was bare to the touch. Cupping her pussy lips, he slid a finger between her slit, watching her open up, and he disappeared within her.

Latching onto her clit, he sucked it into his mouth.

She cried out, her hands on the tile behind her as he brought her closer and closer to orgasm.

Her screams echoed around the room, and when she finally came, he pushed three fingers inside her and felt every pulse.

Afterward, he kissed her clit and stood up.

"I can't believe I let you do that," she said, running her fingers over her wet slit.

"You taste good." He licked his lips. He was about to turn the shower off when her fingers gripped his length.

"You're hard as rock, and I'm not about to let you leave this bathroom without dealing with you first." The smile on her lips was tempting as fuck.

The way she sank to her knees, he wasn't about to protest. When her lips wrapped around the head of his cock, he knew he wasn't going to last long. This woman was so fucking amazing. A true lady to the world and a whore in his bedroom. Only, she belonged to him. No one was going to know just how good she was.

He wasn't going to let anyone else know.

There's no way he'd ever allow her to get away.

If she really thought the whores downstairs were any competition, she was so damn wrong.

Her head bobbed up and down on his length. Tangling his fingers in her blonde hair, he wrapped the length around his fist and began to thrust into her mouth. The tip of his cock slid to the back, and she swallowed him down, taking as much of him as she could. When she gagged on him, he pulled out of her mouth, and she flicked her tongue across the vein before taking him again.

She was so close to swallowing his cock.

Whenever it was too deep, she'd pull off him and bob her head up and down on his length. He couldn't handle it.

The pleasure was out of this world.

He patted her head, warning her that he was about to come. She didn't stop though. She kept on sucking him until he filled her mouth, and she swallowed him down.

He saw her throat working his length until she'd milked him dry.

"Fuck, baby, that was the best wake-up call ever."

Before she could respond, they heard the knocking on the door. Bethany was awake, and it was time for church.

Playtime was over.
****

"Your rage didn't last long," Renee said, taking a seat with her on the grass.

Jasmine had set up a blanket beneath the tree. Bethany was asleep, her arms up and her body spread. She'd been crawling all over the grass for well over an hour when exhaustion had hit.

The weather was too nice to take her back up to that room, so she sat with her, reading the book that she'd been trying to last night.

Closing the book, she watched Bethany. The young girl was in the shade, so Jasmine didn't have to worry. Once she was awake, she intended to feed them both lunch.

"It's hard to stay mad at him." Especially when he gave her a nighttime and morning filled with amazing orgasms.

How could a woman have a problem with that?

She couldn't recall ever being so aroused or so needy.

"Ah, I know that face."

"What face?"

"He got to your woman parts and made them his bitch."

Jasmine laughed, trying to smother the sound so Bethany didn't wake up.

"He has not."

"Please, you've got that look on your face that says you had a damn good time last night."

Jasmine heard something in the other woman's voice.

"What's up?"

"Why does there have to be anything up?"

"Because you sound upset?"

"I'm not upset."

"You're not?"

"No."

"Okay."

"I mean, what do I have to be upset about? It's not like my life is on hold while I wait for Bear to get his head out of his ass?" Renee shrugged. "I can't go on dates. I can't have random sex with men that I don't even know, but he can do whatever the hell he wants to."

"You know about last night?" Jasmine asked.

"It doesn't even matter, really. I mean, I don't even know why I let him get away with this. I could sleep with anyone here, to be honest. That would teach him."

"You're hurt."

Renee had tears in her eyes. "I'm not hurt."

"What is it then?" she asked.

"I'm angry that I let him have this power over me. That I believed for even a second we could have a chance."

Jasmine didn't like seeing her new friend unhappy. Wrapping her arms around her, she pulled her close. "Please don't let him do this. He's not worth it. No man is worth it."

"I look at those skanks and I wonder what it is

that they have that I don't, you know?"

"You shouldn't think that way."

"What do you think I should do?"

She'd never been in this position before. She didn't know what advice to offer.

Tucking her hair behind her ears, she looked out over the garden. This was off the main clubhouse.

Several of the other women were dressed in bikinis, showing off a great deal of their bodies.

She knew Hawk and several of the men weren't at the club today. After their church meeting, they'd taken off. He'd stopped her and Bethany in the kitchen. His only comment was to say he had a few errands to run and he'd be back as soon as they were done.

Jasmine didn't have a clue what errands he had to run.

"Maybe when all this is over with the lockdown and stuff like that we can go out. You know, have that girly day you talked about?" she asked.

She'd never been much of a drinker or a partier. Just one look at Renee and she knew her friend needed some help.

"You'd do that with me?"

"Of course. I'd have to get Hawk to agree because of Bethany, but I'll go out with you." She had no intention of finding a date for herself. "Have you ever thought about asking the other old ladies if they want to go and have some fun?" An idea was forming inside her head. It would be fun for all of them to get out. Get to know each other.

"I haven't."

Bethany gave a little moan. "Why don't you go and ask them while I deal with the little angel?"

"Sure. Sure."

She watched Renee go and turned her attention

on Bethany. The young girl gave a bit of wiggle and a stretch, making her laugh at her antics. She did find her to be so adorable. Once she was sure she was awake, she picked her up and settled her between her legs.

Glancing off toward Renee, she saw the other woman was talking it out with several of the old ladies.

When Bethany started to fuss, she knew it was time to get some food.

"Are you hungry, little baby? Yeah, you hungry? I'm hungry too." She carried her into the kitchen, putting her in the high chair as she found some berries that she could start to feed her.

Bethany was no longer happy with mushed-up banana, and finding food that she actually liked was proving rather difficult. She was used to picky eaters, but Bethany was a challenge for sure.

She had tried mashed potatoes, but that hadn't worked, and neither had any other mashed fruits.

Putting some of the berries into a blender, she pureed them up with a tiny bit of Greek yogurt. Giving the mixture a taste, she added some maple syrup to sweeten it up, and then served.

With the bowl full, she sat down before Bethany, and let the girl have a try.

She had that cute look on her face that said she wasn't happy.

"When you're much older I'll make you all the cheeseburgers you could want."

That seemed to appease her.

Bethany took a couple of spoons of the whizzed-up fruit just as Renee entered the kitchen.

"We've got a girls' night planned. One week after lockdown. They're already getting babysitters on standby."

"I'm going to have to clear it with Hawk first, but

I don't see it being a problem." She gave a little shrug. "This could be a lot of fun. Will we go dancing?"

"We're going where there's lots of booze and men. I don't care about the dancing."

"We must find somewhere that has dancing. I refuse to not dance. I want to go dancing."

"Fine. Fine. We'll find some place that has dancing."

"That's what I'm talking about." She offered Renee a smile.

The plan of it sounded like a lot of fun. She, however, doubted that Hawk would be happy about it.

Chapter Nine

Hawk drew his fist back and slammed it against the Prez of the MC that had been planning on taking him down. This morning, they'd gotten the intel from his lookouts that they were on the move.

The abandoned garage had been completely empty, and with one of his boys tailing the crew, they discovered it was just ten men.

It hadn't taken much in the way of planning to catch up with them. They'd created an ambush and been close enough to this abandoned barn that he didn't even have to worry about doing too much in the way of cleanup. One of his boys had already disposed of the bikes down a damn cliff.

Now he was getting his revenge on the men that nearly took his woman and kid away from him.

This had all been for turf. The Satan's Rulers MC had the turf, and these pieces of shit wanted what belonged to him.

There was no way he was going to let that stand. Not on his watch.

Just thinking about Jasmine passed out on the doctor's table filled him with a rage he wasn't accustomed to.

Over and over, he slammed his fist against the Prez.

When the other man was down for the count, Hawk stepped back.

"Are you sure you're okay, boss?" Bear asked.

"I'm fine, Bear. I've never been better." He paced the length of the barn, coming back to stare at the piece of shit.

The drive-by was supposed to have led him to Stones's crew so they'd fight each other, only it hadn't worked out like that. They'd left the garage and intended to flee when they realized their plan wasn't working.

Five of the ten men were already dead.

The other four were strung up in the barn, most of them knocked out. Red had already taken a piss on all four men while some of Hawk's other men had used them for punching bags.

"This is personal to him," Red said. "Jasmine got shot, and if she'd been holding Bethany any other way, he could have taken out the girl."

Grabbing an old wooden rake, he drew it up and slammed it against the man's skull.

No one, fucking no one, hurt his woman and kid.

Simple as that.

By the end of the beating, no one would ever be able to recognize the Prez.

The two Prospects that had been tailing them finished dousing the barn in gasoline. Flicking his lighter on and off, he stared at the barn. All the bodies were inside. The five dead ones and the five alive ones. The four men strung up couldn't break free, and the Prez was still alive.

This was payback because no one took from him, not like this.

Throwing his lighter onto the gasoline, he stood back and watched as the barn started to go up in flames.

He knew he'd have his revenge on the men who tried to kill him.

If it had just been him, he'd have shown them some mercy and killed them quickly.

They didn't just put his life at risk though, so there was no mercy and it wouldn't be fast either.

He didn't climb on his bike and ride away. He stood there waiting, listening as the men who were still alive screamed for help.

This was why he was Prez.

He made the decisions none of the boys were willing to make.

Finally, after the screams died down and the barn was raging, he straddled his bike and headed back to the clubhouse.

He was covered in blood, and he hoped that he got to sneak in and take a quick shower before Jasmine caught sight of him. She wouldn't exactly be thrilled to see him covered in another man's blood.

Arriving back at the clubhouse, the night was still quite young, and he saw several of the whores dancing naked in the back yard.

A couple of old ladies were not impressed and were glaring at them.

He wasn't interested in dealing with bitch drama. Looking at Red and Bear, he nodded to the action.

"Clean that shit up."

This was another thing that he loved about being Prez. He didn't have to deal with shit jobs like that.

Heading inside, no one rushed toward him, or even stopped him as he went straight toward the bedrooms. Taking them two at a time, he hoped to avoid Jasmine, only she was wrapped in a towel as he entered the room.

Shit.

"Hawk?" Her eyes widened when she took him in. "What the hell happened to you?"

"You don't have to worry about this. It's not my blood." He closed the door and was about to brush past her, but she stopped him with her hands on his jacket.

"Not your blood? What happened? Whose blood is it? What is going on?"

"This is one of those moments when you don't get to ask me questions, babe. I can't give you an answer.

Let me go and clean up."

She nibbled her lip, and he watched as she nodded.

This was going to cause a shitstorm.

He didn't look at his reflection as he knew it was bad.

The state he left the Prez in, it had to be bad. Removing his leather cut, he dropped it to the floor. Next, he tossed his clothes onto the floor. He'd set fire to them and clean his jacket in a moment.

Climbing into the shower, he turned the water on.

The cold hit his flesh. He didn't try to warm it. He took the cold until it finally warmed up. Closing his eyes, he saw the pummeled face and body of the man he'd left close to death but allowed the fire to finish off.

He'd wanted that son of a bitch to suffer, and he had.

The water running down into the drain finally stopped being red and turned clear. Soaping up his body, he saw his knuckles were decorated in cuts that would heal in time.

Turning off the shower, he opened the curtain and there on the toilet sat Jasmine, his leather cut on her lap.

"You killed a man today?"

"I killed several men today."

"Retaliation?"

"Do you really want to know this, or is this just going to make it easier for you to come up with a lame-ass excuse to not fuck me anymore?" After going on a run or doing something like this, he was used to being left alone. This was all new to him, having to deal with the fallout. Having a woman who looked so sad as she held his leather cut.

"You think this is easy for me?"

"You don't get to look at me with those judgey

eyes and think you know shit about me. Yes, I killed a lot of men today in retaliation. You think I was just going to let them get away with harming you? Not going to happen. No one hurts me and mine. You can't handle that, then you're fucked because I'm not letting you go."

He gritted his teeth, hating this moment.

The last thing he wanted to see was tears in her eyes.

"This is who I am. I'm not going to change it. If I didn't do what I did today, then other clubs would come. More men. They won't just stop at shooting shit up. They'll hurt. They'll kill. This is about protecting you and mine. I'm not willing to risk your safety or my daughter's life."

She tucked some hair behind her ears, and he waited for whatever was about to spill from her lips.

"You look tired. I made a nice, big pot of beef casserole. I'm going to warm up your biscuits. If you want to get dressed, I'll meet you downstairs."

In the next second she was gone, and he had to wonder if he'd been talking to himself. Running fingers through his wet hair, he glanced over at the mirror. He looked dazed.

In a way he was.

He expected Jasmine to scold him or to tell him he shouldn't have done the shit he had done.

This was even more confusing to him.

He didn't know what to make of it, and that was irritating him.

Leaving the bathroom, he got dressed and decided against making her wait.

He checked in the nursery to see his baby girl already asleep. With the danger gone, lockdown would be over tomorrow. All the families could go home, and life could get on as normal.

Several of his men nodded at him as he moved through the main clubhouse. He didn't stop to have a beer or to shoot the shit.

They all knew he liked to be alone during these times.

Entering the kitchen, he saw it was empty, apart from him and Jasmine. She'd put out a large bowl of beef casserole. The scent of freshly-baked bread filled the air, and his mouth watered.

His stomach growled as he took a seat.

He scooped up the first mouthful and moaned as the flavors exploded on his tongue. He'd finished his first bowl as she brought over a cup of coffee. She took his empty bowl and refilled it.

The second portion he ate slower, his hunger easing.

She sat down across the table from him, and he waited to look at her.

Neither of them spoke for so long he wondered if she'd fallen asleep.

Glancing up, he saw that she was waiting.

"Say what you need to say," he said.

"Renee's organized a night out with the girls. I want to go with them."

"We're on lockdown," he said. If he had to extend it, he would.

"I've already heard the guys and old ladies talking. It's over tomorrow. We're wanting a girls' night. I want to go with them and seeing as I've not had a day off and I've given you plenty of warning, I'd like to go with them."

"You want to hang out with the old ladies?"

"Yes. I think it would be fun."

He nodded, finding it funny.

"I'm an old lady now, so you say. I think it's right

us ladies get together. We've been stuck here for a few days, and I want to have some fun."

"What do you consider fun?"

"I have no intention to drink, but I love dancing."

"I'll take you dancing."

"Not going to happen. It's going to be girls' night, and that means no boys. It's not fair to Renee that she has to wait around for Bear. She's going to have a good time. Maybe find a guy for the night." She shrugged her shoulder. "I'm not asking for permission. You got to do what you've got to do for the club, and I will accept that on the one condition that when I want to go out with the girls, I can. Be it partying or shopping."

He tilted his head to the side. "You know who you belong to?"

"Yes. I won't be there for other men."

"And I get no say in this?"

"Only if I get a say in what happened upstairs."

"Not happening."

"Then no, you don't."

"I can't change your mind?"

"Nope."

"Then I guess I'll have to deal with it." He was also going to have a word with Bear as well. There's no way he was going to let this become a regular thing.

****

"Come on, barkeep. We need more beers," Renee said. She slapped the counter, shouting for attention.

Jasmine forced a smile to her lips and tried to ignore the glares they were all getting from other customers. There were fifteen of them tonight. She was the designated driver for herself, Renee, and four other women. They had worked out a system and were already planning the next couple of months' worth of ladies' nights. She was happy to go on ladies' night.

Hawk hadn't been happy, but it wasn't her job to not have a life anymore.

A week ago, he'd shocked her completely. After she left the bedroom, wanting very much to storm out of the clubhouse and never see him again, Bear and Red had cornered her. They warned her that after a day where Hawk had to deal with some unpleasantness, he liked to be left alone. They didn't exactly use that language, but it was what they meant in a nutshell. Hawk kills for a day, leave him be. He's a moody bastard. So she'd gone and served him food rather than leaving him alone.

"What are you having to drink?" Renee asked.

"Just a tonic water with a slice of lemon."

Renee laughed. "I can see why Hawk likes you."

"Why?"

"You've got that prim lady thing going. I bet he loves getting that all dirty."

She hoped she wasn't blushing, thinking about all the ways he liked to make her dirty.

The moment the bartender passed her a drink, Renee downed it within a matter of seconds. Sipping at her tonic water, Jasmine waited as Renee ordered another drink. Only this time, they carried their drinks over to their table.

Several of the old ladies were already on the floor dancing. Taking a seat, Jasmine watched as the women looked around the bar, clearly wanting fresh meat.

"Why are they wearing the leather cuts?" she asked, pointing at the women.

"It's the way the men deal with them being out without them. They have to wear their patch. You've got a give a guy some respect that comes and tries anything on with them. Taking on a Satan's Rulers MC old lady is no joke." Renee burst out laughing.

She and Renee didn't have jackets on.

"This is so much fun," one of the women squealed.

"Yeah, so much better than waiting for one of them to come home. I don't see what those bitches do. He comes home, barks out orders, farts, and passes out," another of the women said.

"I don't like it. I don't like any of it," Renee said. "No matter who I go out with or even if I try to date in another town, Bear's always there. He's always ruining everything. I hate him." Renee swallowed her drink. "I'm dancing. Come on."

Jasmine was pulled onto the dance floor and dancing within a matter of seconds. Letting the beat wash over her, she watched Renee as the other woman started to loosen up.

"This is just what I needed. Time away from that asshole to be myself." She let out a whoop and looking past her shoulder, Jasmine saw a couple of men waiting to swoop in.

She danced with Renee, keeping an eye on their table, and of course more of the old ladies decided they'd had enough of waiting for their men who left them at home most times, and started to dance.

For some reason she couldn't help but worry that if the women allowed these men who were not part of the MC to think they had a shot, this was going to be bad news.

"Do you think we should be letting other men dance with us?" Jasmine asked.

Renee cupped her face. "Relax. These ladies have wanted a chance to get back at their men. They're sitting in their clubhouse, getting their dick sucked and all they have to do is crook their finger and the women come to them. It's our time now. Girls' night is going to be so popular. I love this already. Come on, Jasmine. Stop worrying so much. This is supposed to be fun."

Throwing caution to the wind, Jasmine let herself go, basking in the heat of the night and the enjoyment of the music.

Chapter Ten

Hawk ran Bethany's child monitor across his lip and back. She was down for the night in the clubhouse nursery where many of the kids were. He sat in the main clubhouse room, waiting for his woman to come home. He'd ordered her to come back to the clubhouse. Glancing around the room, he saw several of the men whose women were out tonight had the same thought.

A couple of them didn't seem to care and were flirting with the club whores to keep themselves entertained.

He wasn't happy.

He didn't like her being out there on her own.

Since lockdown had ended, business had returned to normal, but when he got home, he didn't let Jasmine go to her own room.

She was in his bed every single night, and he'd gotten the pleasure of playing with her body just the way he wanted.

There's no way he'd ever risk Jasmine for one of these women. They bounced from cock to cock because it was their job to do and they loved it.

"You're looking ready to kill," Bear said, taking a seat at his table.

"The reason most of the women are out tonight is your fault."

"Fuck off. None of this shit is on me."

"It is. Renee is sick and tired of you getting to live your own life, and that's why she arranged everything. The women coming, the night out. She wants to get over you by finding herself a man that has nothing to do with you."

Bear's cheek tensed up. "That shit ain't happening."

"For all you know Renee could be being fucked against a wall right now. Five men lining up to see just how good of a pussy she's got." Hawk watched and waited.

"She's mine."

"Yeah, and you're not claiming shit. I doubt she'd even want your dick now. It's seen one too many whores for her taste. What she needs is a nice, fresh dick that looks at her and only her."

"Fuck this shit. No one is having her. She's mine." Bear slammed the chair across the room.

"Where are you going?" Hawk asked.

"I'm done waiting. I'm going after what's mine."

Hawk smiled and tossed Bethany's speaker to one of the men. "Keep an ear out for her. She should be down for the count."

"Where are you going?" one of the men asked.

"I'm going to get my woman."

He walked out of the clubhouse, going toward his bike. Bear was already out of the grounds, and he couldn't help but smile. Nothing like the thought of another pair of balls swinging in your woman's face to make that claim.

Straddling his bike, he rode out of the parking lot, heading toward the bar Jasmine had told them they were going to.

Gunning the engine, he took each bend, and it didn't take him long to find Bear who was a few feet in front of him.

They arrived at the bar within a matter of minutes, breaking several rules along the way.

Bear climbed off his bike, and Hawk grabbed his arm. "You've got to play this cool."

"Fuck cool. She knows who she belongs to."

"Does she? Or is this another point where you

take her home, come back to the clubhouse, and screw other women?"

"Why do you care so much?"

"Because if you step in there and ruin this for her, I've got a feeling she won't be coming around anymore, and as much as you keep her at arm's length, you like her. Make your mind up. Renee's either yours or she's not, but she can't be both and you can't keep ruining every single guy for her. She has a chance to find someone." He wouldn't usually interfere with the guys' lives like this, but Bear and Renee had been dancing around each other for some time now.

He had to do something, especially if they were about to go in there and stake their own claim on their women.

"She's mine."

"She's yours?"

"Yeah, I want her, and no one's taking her away from me." With Bear's mind made up, they entered the bar, and it took Hawk a few seconds to find his woman.

She looked beautiful in the dress she wore but stood out like a sore thumb. The pretty floral summer dress only enhanced the innocent look that she had. Her blue eyes were closed as she swayed to the music. Renee was in front of her, but the other woman had another man wrapped all around her.

No one touched Jasmine, and he was more than okay with that.

Leaving Bear to deal with his own problem, he walked right up to his woman, admiring the curve of her ass. A couple of men who were partying the night away admired his woman. He wasn't about to ruin her night by slitting their throats, but he wanted to. When it came to Jasmine, she brought out his protective side.

The wound on her shoulder was healing up

nicely, and she no longer looked in pain when she had to lift something. Wrapping an arm around her waist, he pressed his lips to her ear. She started to struggle, but the moment he spoke, she relaxed.

"Hey, baby, you look pretty lonely all by yourself."

"I wasn't lonely." She looked toward Renee, who was now in Bear's arms. They were sharing heated words as they danced.

Spinning Jasmine around into his arms, he smiled down at her. "You're lonely now."

"What are you doing here?"

"I was making sure Bear didn't make an ass of himself."

"He should be begging her for forgiveness."

"A little birdie tells me that Renee is going to get everything her heart desires, including the man she's been panting after."

Jasmine put her hands around his neck, her body flush against his. The lady was still in charge.

He'd noticed whenever they were not alone or in the bedroom, Jasmine didn't give anything away. He loved this about her.

She knew without a doubt who she belonged to.

"Did you miss me?" Jasmine asked.

"I did."

"Who is looking after Bethany?"

"One of the boys."

"You know this was supposed to be a girls' night."

"It was, and now it's an 'our night.'" He ran his hands down her body, cupping her generous ass. "And I intend to make sure that the only thing you remember about this night is me."

"Well, you've got a lot to do, because I've only

been drinking tonic water. I'm perfectly aware of everything."

"How about we skip this part and head home? I can show you a good time in my bedroom."

She chuckled. "I'd love to, but I can't. I'm the designated driver, and I'm not going to let my girls down. They wanted to come out tonight, and no men should be allowed." She cupped his face, and he tilted her head back, taking possession of her lips. Sliding his leg between hers, he drew it up so that she was dancing across his leg.

Jasmine pulled back from the kiss, but he saw the hunger in her eyes. She wanted him.

"You don't want to continue fucking my leg?"

"Hawk, please."

"Please, what? Fuck you?"

"I want you."

But she also wanted to stay to help. He got it, and he fucking admired it. She wasn't willing to leave the women here, and for that, he fucking adored her.

With his fingers wrapped around her wrist, he didn't care who saw them. Leaving the bar, he rounded the building and pressed her up against the brick. Taking her hands in his, he held them above her head.

"Now you're completely at my mercy."

He pressed his cock against her, and she moaned.

Sliding a hand beneath her dress, he cupped her pussy through the fabric, feeling just how wet she was. She soaked his fingers from the first touch.

Tearing her panties from her body, he pushed her dress up to her waist. He released her hands to lift her up.

"Take my cock out." He had his woman in his hands. She loosened his belt and pulled out his cock. He released a hiss as the pleasure was intense. "Put me inside you, babe. I can't wait another second."

She placed the tip of his cock against her clit and slowly eased down until he filled her pussy. They both cried out as he filled her inch by inch. Holding onto her waist, he slammed her down on his cock until he was at the hilt. Her hands went to his shoulders, and against the wall, she started to work his cock as he held her in place, moving his dick inside her at the same time.

The music was dull, and all he could hear was their heavy breathing.

Over and over again, he fucked her, making her his, taking what belonged to him, and she did belong. This woman was all his, and he was never letting her go, not ever.

Jasmine was a fucking treasure and only a blind asshole couldn't see it.

Pounding inside her, they both cried out as he flooded her pussy with his release. They were both panting, and he let go of her ass, holding her against the wall as he sank his fingers into her hair, pulling her down for a kiss.

This woman had ruined him for anyone else.

****

Jasmine dropped off the last of the old ladies and instead of driving to the clubhouse, she went home. Those were Hawk's instructions. He'd already gotten someone to take care of Bethany, and even though she felt guilty for leaving the young girl, she wanted the time with Hawk.

Soon reality would come crashing down around her, and she wouldn't have any excuse for spending time with him. The agency would find out, and then she'd be off their books for good.

Part of her was afraid of that.

Pulling up onto the drive, she climbed out and made her way inside.

She went straight upstairs to their bedroom.

Hawk wouldn't let her sleep anywhere but in his bed.

Everything was moving so fast and yet not fast enough.

They fucked all the time, but that wasn't it. They talked all the time about everything and nothing. There were moments where she found herself thinking about him coming back bloody with that look in his eye, but she must have been dropped as a baby or something because it didn't last very long and then she was thinking about the future with him, about what it could mean.

Could she be his old lady?

Taking care of Bethany?

She loved that little girl so much.

Taking a seat on the edge of the bed, she removed her shoes and took off her dress. She heard the door open and close, and she waited with bated breath for him to arrive.

Completely naked, she sat on the edge of the bed, her legs spread, sitting back on her hands, waiting for him. This was how he wanted her to wait.

She was all his to do with as he pleased.

When he rounded the corner and he stood in the doorway, her pussy tightened. He wore his leather cut. His hair was wild as she'd run her fingers through it many times on the dance floor. After they fucked against the wall, they'd gone back inside and danced until it was time to leave.

"Did everyone make it home safe?" he asked.

"Yes."

"Good." He removed his leather cut. "Come here."

She stepped off the bed and walked up to him. He held the jacket out for her to try on. She put her hands into the cut, and he placed it on her shoulders.

"From now on when you go out, you wear this. No man will ever be allowed to touch or take what is mine." He wrapped his arms around her, pulling her close.

She loved it when he went all possessive and didn't like to share her with anyone else. He slid his hands inside the jacket and cupped her tits. He gave them a squeeze before teasing the nipples. As he tugged on the hardened tips, arousal flooded her pussy.

"Bend over the bed," he said.

She did as he asked, glancing over her shoulder.

He stepped up behind her, spreading the cheeks of her ass. His fingers teased through her slit, plunging inside her, drawing back to stroke her puckered hole.

She moaned as he circled her anus before pressing against it.

His cock was at her entrance within the next second, and she cried out at the width of him as he slammed balls deep within her. She felt them slap against her pussy.

Closing her eyes, she felt him stroke her ass, pressing inside until he could get a finger, which he moved to the knuckle.

He began to thrust that single digit in and out of her anus, getting her used to the intrusion, in and out until she was begging for more. The burn stopped but started again as he added a second to her ass, stretching her open.

Sliding a hand between her thighs, she started to stroke her clit, crying out as he pounded away inside her. She loved it when he fucked her.

Only this time, Hawk stopped. He pulled out of her and moved her up the bed so that she was on her back. He held her knees up close to her chest and from the angle he had her, it was the perfect position for his cock.

"Hold your knees."

She watched as he held his dick and placed it at her anus. He was slick with both of their cum, and she cried out as inch by inch he sank inside her.

The burn was intense, and he waited for her to get accustomed to the first inch before sliding in the second.

She'd never felt so full, and as she tried to push him out, Hawk slid in deeper until the entire length of his cock was deep within her ass.

"Fuck, that is a pretty sight." He gave her pussy a little slap, his fingers sliding across her clit, stroking her. "I can feel how tight you are. Your ass holding my dick, wanting it." He pulled out of her and started to rock inside her.

She glanced down between them, watching his cock as he filled her, going in and out, in and out.

"I want you to come. Let me feel your tight ass wrapped around my dick." He didn't stop stroking her.

The pleasure began to build, and even as she gritted her teeth, wanting it to last, there was no way for it.

He brought her to orgasm, and she screamed his name as he started to rock back inside her. His cock seeming to thicken as he filled her.

After her release, he held her legs, keeping her wide open as he fucked her ass.

"Watch me, Jasmine. Your ass is mine. All fucking mine."

He rode her ass, and she knew she belonged to him.

There was no denying it. He was hers just as she belonged to him.

"Oh, fuck, you're so fucking good. Such a dirty

girl. *My* dirty girl."

His orgasm neared, and when he thrust inside her a final time, she felt every wave of his cum as he filled her ass.

She closed her eyes as the pleasure rippled through her.

Hawk pumped inside her, groaning one final time as he changed positions. His cock was still in deep, but his hands wrapped around her. He stroked her stomach, kissing her neck, sucking on the pulse.

She felt happy.

Stroking his arms, she stared across the room. Part of her expected him to be asleep, but he kept on kissing her neck.

"Talk to me, babe," he said.

"What's there to say?"

"What you're thinking about right now."

"My ass is a little sore." She looked behind her. He was staring right at her. His arms tightened around her waist. "That was amazing."

"You're amazing, Jasmine."

She nibbled her lip. "I've never been like this with anyone before."

"What do you mean?"

"The way I'm with you. The sex. The dirty talk. I've never been like that. Not even with my ex-husband."

She didn't know why she was telling him this.

"You weren't hot like this in the bedroom?"

Jasmine shook her head. "You probably don't believe me."

He cupped her cheek tilting her head back. "I believe you. I've no reason to doubt you."

"I … when I'm with you it's like I can't help myself. It scares me. I don't … I only want you, Hawk. With my ex, it was always one position, and it was so boring. I think I fell asleep a couple of times during it. I'd wake up to him snoring, and I was so unsatisfied. It was hard for me to tell him what I wanted. What I craved. I think it's why our marriage started to fall apart. I couldn't tell him the truth, and he didn't know what was wrong with me."

"There's nothing wrong with you. He just wasn't man enough to handle the kind of woman you are, but I know who you are. I see you, and there's no way I'd let another man touch what's mine." He kissed her hard. "Don't think for a second that I'll share you, baby. I never will. What we have. What we share, to me that is a fucking treasure, and I'm not going to let you go. Not now. Not ever." He kissed her again, and she moaned. "Fuck, your ass is so tight. You want to be fucked again, don't you?"

He cupped her tits, and she arched up into his touch, wanting him, begging for him, needing only him.

This was what scared her a lot. This wasn't just about sex.

She was starting to fall for Hawk, and if this was only sex for him, then she was screwed.

Chapter Eleven

One week later

"Prez, you heard a word I said?" Red asked.

Hawk looked up at his two men who were waiting for a response. He'd be calling church soon as they had another gun run to attend to. They were driving them across the state to hand over to the cartel for the war they were having on the streets. He should be thinking about the plan and how to execute it so his men didn't get caught.

Gun runs were always tricky as there was a higher risk of the law following their tracks, which was why planning was always key in these assignments. He didn't want any of his men in jail for something like this. If any of them ended up in jail it meant deals had to be made to help with protection.

Running a hand down his face, he tried to clear his head. He shouldn't be thinking about Jasmine at a time like this. The woman had gotten under his skin, and now he couldn't fucking focus.

"Sorry, start from the top."

"There's a lot of heat coming straight off the docks. We're thinking bringing them back to the clubhouse, changing trucks, and then following this down the state line, taking back routes rather than main roads. Less traffic, less heat, and an easy deal," Red said.

He checked across the map and stared at the path. It was one they'd done many times, but he didn't like changing vehicles at the clubhouse. That brought too much heat home, and he wasn't willing to do that.

Finding a location along the way, he pointed at it. "We have our boys wait here. It's secure and covered. We change vehicles, and carry on with the mission. We don't have anyone in town talking about a big truck that pulled into the Satan's Rulers MC and then cops are flooding the place."

"The sounds right, Prez," Bear said.

Ever since he'd claimed Renee—and he had claimed her—she wore the old lady jacket and even Bear's ring, even though it wasn't an engagement ring. It was just a ring that Bear always wore. It was his symbol of affection and ownership to her—the fucker had been happy.

It was about time.

Hawk had also heard a couple of the bitches talking that they weren't happy Bear wasn't interested in them anymore.

When a guy fell for a woman, the whores lost power within the club.

He thought about Jasmine. He wondered if she knew the agency had been in touch with him and had organized a meeting. He didn't want to worry her.

She loved her job, not that taking care of Bethany was a job for her. He saw her as his daughter's mother more than even her biological mother.

Running fingers through his hair, he sat back. "That's what we're going to do."

"Prez, you okay?" Red asked.

"Fine."

"Look, these gun runs are a piece of piss so long as everyone's head's in the game. We need to know you're with us here," Red said.

"It's about Jasmine, isn't it?" Bear asked, taking a seat.

"I'm not a pussy. I'm not going to spill out my thoughts to you guys."

"We could help," Red said. "Give you advice."

"I don't need advice." He wasn't about to talk about his feelings or that he was in love with Jasmine.

Fuck!

Even to himself, he sounded like a pussy.

"We're not leaving until you talk," Bear said.

"I could make you."

"Yeah, and then you'd be sitting alone in this big office thinking about Jasmine. That's who you're thinking about," Red said. "No need to deny it. Everyone can see how smitten you are with your woman."

"I don't need to hear this shit."

"Why not?" Bear asked. "I pushed Renee away, and it was the craziest thing I ever did."

"You've been with her an entire week. Relationships get tricky, Bear. They get hard."

"And how much harder can they get? My woman knows I'm here with women I fucked. You think I don't get a hard time over that shit? I've got to make it up to her." Bear shrugged. "I'm willing to do what needs to be done for her to know I mean business."

"Jasmine's a tough cookie," Red said. "She can handle whatever you throw at her."

"You don't know her."

"The night you took out that other MC. You set fire to the barn, and we listened to them scream. It was your decision. You always like to be alone, and you'd gone up to your room and Jasmine came down. We told her not to worry. That you need to be by yourself during that time. She went into the kitchen and served you dinner. She adapted for you. I imagine she was hurt by whatever you said to her. She's not going to run from you. She'd stand and fight by your side. She's a strong woman."

"I want to marry her," he said, shocking even himself with that revelation.

"Do you want to do this before or after the run, because weddings take a lot?" Bear said.

"Aren't you worried?" Red asked.

"Why would I be worried?"

"Hate to break it to you, but Renee and Jasmine are tight. You could be walking down the aisle before you know it."

"Renee doesn't want to get married," Bear said.

Hawk and Red chuckled.

"I fucking hate you two."

Bear got to his feet and left the room. Staring out the window, Hawk looked out over the clubhouse.

"You could do worse."

"I have done worse." He thought about Bethany's mom. He'd had no problems putting that woman to ground. She'd been a piece of shit.

"If you can't live without her then you're going to have to make a decision." Red got to his feet. "I'll organize the teams for the drop off and pick up. You'll make the right decision."

Red left his office, and he ran a hand down his face.

This thing between him and Jasmine, it wasn't going away.

Getting to his feet, he left the clubhouse, and went straight to his bike. Straddling it, he took off, heading home. What he needed was a long ride, but he didn't want to be away from his woman.

Pulling up outside of his home, he saw Jasmine's car still in the driveway complete with Bethany's car seat in the back.

His woman was home.

Entering the house, he didn't hear her. Going to the back where the kitchen was, he caught sight of her in the yard on the grass with Bethany on the blanket. She was smiling as she held Bethany. His little girl was taking one step and then another.

He covered his mouth and gasped as Jasmine held up a cell phone and was filming it.

"We've got to show your daddy what a big girl you are. Yes, you are. That's it. Look at you, Bethany. Such a big girl."

Stepping out of the back door, Jasmine looked over at him and smiled. "You saw?"

"I saw."

"I got it on camera, but she's walking."

Bethany sat on the ground and clapped her hands.

Picking her up, he held her close, seeing that she was growing up so fast. He kissed her cheek, and Jasmine got to her feet. "Do you want a drink?" she asked. "Are you staying? I don't know if you were just stopping by?"

"I'm staying. How about we go out for dinner? You, me, and Bethany."

"I'd love that. She doesn't scream as much."

He didn't care if his girl screamed the entire time.

This was his family.

Him, Jasmine, and Bethany.

Jasmine went to walk away, and he caught her hand, pulling her to him.

"What is it?"

"I killed her."

"What?"

"Bethany's mother was a traitor. She was about to sell out the club, and she was leaving Bethany all day by herself to fend for herself." He stopped. "I killed her."

"Why are you telling me this?" Jasmine asked.

"Because I need you to know that this for me is real. That I want this with you. The way you take care of Bethany, I know you won't hurt her. You care about her."

"I love her."

"Her real mom didn't. She couldn't give a shit. She left her here alone. Off fucking whoever would have her, trying to sell out the club."

Tears filled Jasmine's eyes, and she stared at Bethany. "I wouldn't do that. I wouldn't sell out the club."

"I'm not a good person."

"You are. You're a good person that does bad things." She stroked Bethany's cheek and then kissed his cheek. "Do you want me to leave? Is that why you're telling me?"

"No, I don't want you to go."

"I'm not going then," she said. "You've got me, and I'm not going away until you kick me out."

She swiped away the tears. "I'll get you that drink."

He watched her walk into his house.

He was screwed.

When it came to Jasmine, he wasn't going to be able to walk away.

He didn't want to.

****

Jasmine didn't feel so good. The visit from the agency didn't go very well, and as she sat at the dinner table with her notice of being let go, she felt like the biggest fucking failure in the world. They had been made aware of her relationship with Hawk Dark and were not happy that she'd abused her position. There had been a supervisor from the agency who'd decided to do a silent check on her. He'd caught her with Hawk and reported her immediately. Even though it was her first offense they didn't believe in offering second chances.

From that day forward, her contracts had been terminated and she was permanently removed from the books.

Biting her lip, everything seemed to come crashing down around her. It had been only a couple of months with Hawk, but now, her life, the possibilities, were all gone. That little girl upstairs taking a nap meant the world to her. Hawk, damn it, for all of his brash biker ways, she fucking loved him.

What was she going to do now without a job? Would they send another nanny?

She felt sick to her stomach and so sad over everything.

What if this was just a bit of fun for him?

He'd declared her as his old lady, but did that really have any meaning at all? She wiped at her nose and got to her feet as she heard the door open.

"Babe, you won't believe the day I've had. First Bear and Renee called me this morning and told me they eloped. That they're not waiting around to get married."

She forced a smile to her lips as he came into the dining room.

He took one look at her and then at the table. "What's up?"

"It's nothing. Renee called me. She said she'd throw a party or we could have a girls' night. She sounded excited."

Hawk picked up the letter off the table.

"I had a meeting with them tomorrow," he said, looking at it.

"Well, you don't have to worry. They have already fired me, and they're well within their rights. I broke all of their rules." It was the first time ever she'd ever broken so many rules. "I've never done anything like this before." She ran fingers through her hair and took a step back.

"Never?"

"No. I've never crossed any lines or boundaries.

I've been a nanny and that's all. That's all I wanted to be. All I needed to be and I've never felt that I needed to change that." She blew out a breath. "I can't even believe I've done this now. I mean, what is happening to me?"

"Are you in love with me?" Hawk asked.

Her gaze went to his. "Excuse me?"

"It's pretty simple. Do you love me or not?"

"Hawk?"

"If you don't, I get it. I'm a single dad. I've got a kid that when you first met her wouldn't stop crying. I'm a Prez. I do a lot of bad shit to a lot of people. I've even admitted some of what I do, and I'm not willing to change. I *can't* change. This is who I am, but I know that there isn't any other woman in this world that can make me feel so fucking afraid and excited all at the same time."

She frowned, looking at him. "What?"

"When I'm with you, no one else exists. It's just you and me, and I couldn't give a fuck about anything else in between. You set me on fire, and I'm so fucking afraid that you'll look at me and see me for what I am, and that's a man who doesn't deserve a woman like you. I know I'm lucky, and I'm telling you know, I am completely, one-hundred percent devoted to you. None of the … *other women* appeal to me."

Jasmine couldn't help but smile at his different choice of word for the women of the club.

"I don't promise you that every day is going to be easy, but I do promise you that when times are tough, I'll be by your side. That I won't stop loving you, nor will I stop fucking you and making you scream my name. I will make that my vow to never walk away from an argument, and if I don't like the way it's going, I'll pound your pussy until we're friends again."

This made her laugh. Tears filled her eyes, and

she gasped as he tore up the letter.

"You're not my kid's nanny, and I'm not your boss. You're my woman, Jasmine, and the only people who matter are me and Bethany. Not them. Ignore them. You're my woman through and through, and I will be the one to take care of you. Forever. Now tell me what I want to hear, baby. Tell me."

Staring into his eyes, she knew without a doubt what he wanted to hear.

"I love you too."

He cupped her face and slammed his lips down on hers. This felt so right. She couldn't be in a world that didn't have him in it. He'd awakened a part of her soul and now there was no turning back.

Hawk broke from the kiss. "Wait, wait, let me do this."

She watched as he went down on one knee and held up a ring.

"Hawk?"

"Jasmine Clark, will you do me the honor of becoming my wife?"

"You want to marry me?"

"I want to fucking own every part of you."

"This has to be the most beautiful proposal."

"Is that a yes?"

"Yes, a hell yes."

He slid the ring on her finger, and she cupped his face, kissing him. Just as he lifted her up onto the counter, Bethany's cries came over the speaker.

"Typical," he said. "Girl's a cock block."

Jasmine cupped his face. "It doesn't matter because we've got the rest of our lives to look forward to."

"You're right. Come on, let's go and see our little girl."

Epilogue

Five years later

"Happy anniversary, baby," Hawk said, holding up his beer bottle.

"It has been quite an anniversary," Jasmine said, clinking her water with his bottle. They snuggled in against each other beneath the tree, watching all the kids and the club as they partied. They still only had Bethany. It had taken them some time to finally get pregnant, and as he placed one hand on her stomach, he felt the little sucker kick. Jasmine was eight and a half months along. She wouldn't be able to get up, but he'd help her. He loved being there for her every need. When she got pregnant, she'd freaked out, worried about losing it, but he knew they were going to be fine. They had each other, so nothing else was worth worrying about.

This was one of the reasons they'd stayed home. He could have taken her anywhere, but their place was here, at home, with their family. Also, he'd practiced the route to the hospital so when her waters broke, he could get her there in ten minutes flat. All the boys were on standby for that moment. Running his fingers through her long hair, he smiled.

Five years.

Five fucking years he'd been married to this woman.

"You know, I can still remember that smile on your face when you saw me at the grocery store," he said.

"I was more interested in your screaming baby. I thought you were hot, though."

Bethany was sitting at one of the benches, her hair in ponytails as she drew something in her book.

His little girl was one fine artist. Their house was completely covered in all of her creations.

He'd married Jasmine as soon as it could be arranged, which was within the month. Neither of them wanted a fancy wedding. The club had been present, and that was enough. Jasmine didn't have any family alive, so his club had given her the family she missed out on.

Some of the club whores—no, *other women*—were there, and he was surprised to find out that Jasmine even befriended them. She was nice to everyone, but she had no problem telling a woman to stay away from her man.

He rather liked being Jasmine's property, especially knowing she belonged to him.

They had each other, and that was enough.

"When do we think this little guy is going to pop out?" he asked, touching her swollen stomach.

"Like his daddy, when he's good and ready."

She tilted her head back, and he smiled down at her. "I love you."

"I love you too."

He leaned down and claimed her lips. She released a moan and then a gasp.

"What is it?" he asked.

"Erm, I think he wants to come now. Hawk, my water just broke."

All of his well-laid-out plans … shattered.

The next hour was the longest of his life, and by the time he arrived at the hospital, she had already started to push. With no time to get her to the labor ward, she gave birth in the emergency room.

His little boy arrived on their anniversary, and he knew now there was no way he was ever going to have an excuse not to remember this day, not that he'd ever forget it.

The End

SAM CRESCENT

THE MAFIA'S VIRGIN NANNY

The Nannies, 4

Sam Crescent

Copyright © 2019

Chapter One

"All you do all day is fuck your little whores. You're not even a man." The sound of the slap was more than enough for Tessa Brown. She picked up Caesar and carried him out of the room where his mother was in the process of crying.

She had learned to never get involved with Jessica and Benedict Adesso. They were married, but she didn't understand why. Actually, she knew perfectly well why. Alonzo Zanetti had declared it, and his word was law. Head of the mafia and ruler of those beneath him, his sister had just been another pawn in the game he played. At least, that was what she was told.

Two years into the marriage, and it looked like the couple were no closer to liking each other, even if they had brought into the world Caesar, the beautiful baby boy she nannied for.

Of course, all of this was done under Alonzo's roof. He wouldn't allow them to leave. Did he even have a clue what went on? She doubted it. From seeing Jessica herself, she knew the other woman hid the abuse she suffered with makeup or certain clothes, and it wasn't like Alonzo spent all that much time staring at his sister. The house was large enough for them to have a separate wing, so no one would ever hear Jessica scream.

Holding Caesar on her large hip, Tessa started the walk down the wide staircase. She winced as she heard Jessica call him a bastard and a few other choice words.

Times like this, she wished above everything else that she didn't have this job. Not that she had much choice in the matter.

After her parents died, she'd been taken in by the mafia, as her father had been an important soldier for them. He'd been well-respected, and even though he tried to keep his only daughter out of the line of fire, it didn't happen. Which was why at twenty years old, she worked for the most feared man in the world.

From the moment she'd been employed, at Alonzo's insistence, she'd been told to never be seen or heard. If men or women entered a room, she always vacated it quietly. It helped that she had perfected the art of being invisible. In a world full of violence and women in designer clothes, she didn't exactly fit in. She never wore makeup and wouldn't be caught dead on a treadmill. She was all natural, with large hips, thick thighs, a tummy that was the result of too much ice cream, and tits that were too big.

Even with her size sixteen body, she was able to get around silently. She liked being alone.

The other nanny, Michele, liked to be noticed and would often leave Caesar alone to fuck one of the soldiers. Only, before anyone would miss her, she'd be back, looking like she truly cared for the young boy.

Tessa wasn't interested in relationships or anything else. All she wanted to do was live her life, and to one day maybe make a small home somewhere. If she was lucky enough to have kids, she'd want at least two or three. Four if her husband wanted that.

Still, that seemed like a long way off.

For now, she was content to help take care of Caesar. If she didn't do it, no one else would.

Jessica was a nice woman but at times really jealous. Anytime Benedict would walk into a room, she'd scream at any other woman to get out, even Michele. Fortunately, Jessica knew Tessa wasn't like that, so she didn't get yelled at anymore, which was a relief.

The one thing Tessa couldn't stand more than anything else was getting yelled at. Even when her parents or a teacher was mad at her, it would freeze her into place and she couldn't move. Much to her embarrassment, she'd also cry, which served to make her the object of much humiliation at school.

She hummed to Caesar as he played with the cross she wore around her neck. It was the last gift her parents had given her when she turned eighteen. It was a beautiful silver cross, and she never took it off.

Her father had told her to wear it, that it would keep her safe and help her make good decisions.

Going to school that day had seemed like a good decision. When she came home, Alonzo Zanetti had been waiting for her. It was the last morning she saw her parents, and she had completed her schooling here in the Zanetti mansion before she became Jessica's nanny.

Once she was down the stairs that led to the Adesso wing of the mansion, she came to the top of the stairs that would now take her to the ground floor of the house. Caesar loved being in the library, and as there was so much carpet, she would sit with him for hours. He had his own little box of toys that he would play all day with. Being only one year old, he was still very much a baby, but he liked to crawl around a lot, and he gurgled, which she found so adorable.

Michele would have to find them, but last Tessa saw she was taking one of the guards into a bedroom. She even believed the other nanny had been sleeping with Caesar's father as well, but that was just speculation and she'd never caught them.

Not one to gossip or talk, or do much of anything, Tessa kept her thoughts to herself.

Her father told her the only way to survive in the mafia was to keep your mouth shut and to always look the other way.

She'd never been kept in the dark about what her father really did. They wanted her to know that even though they were part of the mafia, they'd want her to have a normal life. Most soldiers' kids were allowed that luxury.

Right now, she didn't see herself as living a normal life, or any other kind of life.

She was halfway down the stairs, too late to make an escape. Alonzo Zanetti stood there with several of his men. She recognized Cole and Demetri, who were his personal guards. There were also a couple of other men.

She turned on her heel and was about to head back upstairs when Caesar released a little squeal.

She cringed as a quick glance at Caesar clearly showed he wanted his uncle.

"Come down, Tessa," Alonzo said.

The last thing she wanted to do was go down.

Ignoring his request could get her killed. Still,

part of her was tempted to run, only because she'd seen him look so scary at times.

Turning back toward the stairs, she didn't look at him, careful as she made her way to the bottom step.

Alonzo was already there, and as he grabbed Caesar, his hand grazed her breasts. She ignored it though. Biting her lip, she waited, not sure if she should look at him or leave.

"Where is my sister?" Alonzo asked.

She looked up at him. His brown eyes were so dark they looked almost black. His hair was a mess from clearly running his fingers through the long length.

"She's in her quarters," she said.

He sighed. "Benedict?"

"With her."

"Ah, I see. There's nothing like a lovers' quarrel to send you running."

Heat filled her cheeks.

"Where's the other nanny?" he asked.

"I-I don't know."

He sighed. "Cole, go check one of the bedrooms. Please make sure Michele is aware that she's in charge for now, that Tessa is not available at the moment."

"Got it."

"It's fine. I don't mind taking care of Caesar." She didn't want Michele to hate her any more than she already did for some reason.

"I pay you to do a job, and since you came here you've not had any time off. It hasn't gone unnoticed, even if you try to act invisible."

She heard Demetri laugh, and she glanced in his direction.

Caesar chuckled, and Alonzo did the same. "You are a handsome devil, aren't you? Don't worry. You have Zanetti blood inside you. You're going to get all the women when you grow up. They will not be able to resist your charms."

The sound of footsteps had her turning in the direction. Cole had Michele by the arm.

"Our little slut-in-waiting was able to be pried away from the dick she was riding," Alonzo asked.

"I wasn't doing anything wrong. Besides, Caesar was in good hands," Michele said, shooting Tessa a scornful look as if it was her fault she'd been caught.

That wasn't something Tessa was going to take the blame for. Did Alonzo even realize that Michele rarely did her job?

"I have no care about who you fuck, Michele, but do it on your own time. Get back to work. Caesar needs you. He can be in *your* capable hands. Cole and Demetri will make sure you do your job." Alonzo kissed Caesar's head, and then handed the baby over to her. "Now go, or would you like to leave my employment?"

"No, sir."

Tessa chanced a look at Michele, who was already giving her dirty looks as if she'd been the cause of this.

Staring down at the floor, she hoped the ground would open her up and swallow her rather than deal with this woman's wrath.

"Good, go."

"You don't want to come, Tessa?" Michele asked.

"Tessa is busy." Alonzo answered for her, and she hated it but didn't argue.

Locking her fingers together in front of her, she waited.

It was all too soon that they were alone.

****

Alonzo stared at the young woman before him.

He knew she tried to leave whenever he entered a room and that any attention always made her run like a little bunny. She tried to be invisible, but that just wasn't possible.

Not with him.

He noticed her every time he entered a room.

The sweet, floral scent she left behind always drove him crazy. Of course, he never stopped her.

She was a sweet young woman. He'd been the one to see her to deliver the bad news, on her birthday two years ago. She never celebrated her birthday. Louise, their cook, told him that she always declined a cake being made or any cards. In two years, she'd not celebrated her birthday, and she spent a lot of time at the graveyard where her parents were buried.

Since she worked for him, she didn't do any of her studies. She'd graduated high school, but that was it. Before Jessica had her baby, Tessa cleaned his home to make her way.

He couldn't even recall a time she left the mansion unless it was to go and see her parents' graves. Once a year wasn't healthy.

She looked way too pale to him.

"Come with me."

"I don't want to be a bother."

"You're not. Follow me."

She nodded her head, and he held out his hand, which she took. Even if she hadn't placed her hand within his, he'd have made it so.

Simple as.

When it came to Tessa, she was like a different kind of woman, one he didn't really understand.

He was used to women who liked to fuck around. Play mind games.

Tessa didn't have a boyfriend. She was a good

girl.

It's what her father used to say about her whenever he'd show off a picture. His daughter was his pride and joy. In the mafia, the men wanted sons, not girls. Having a daughter wasn't to be celebrated. Not until she proved her use to them by spreading her legs for the right husband.

Maxwell Brown had been different.

For ten years he and his wife had tried for a baby. Much to their disappointment, they hadn't been blessed with children easily. When his wife finally did fall pregnant, Maxwell was like a crazed man.

For nine straight months it was his mission to rid the world of every single evil man he could find, and to make them all pay.

Alonzo couldn't blame him. The world was full of bad people who did bad things, the mafia included.

They didn't want to know the sex of their child, so on the day she was born, it was a surprise.

Alonzo had been at the hospital the day she was born, as had his father. At fifteen years old, he'd known Maxwell's loyalty was greatly respected by his family. They'd do anything for him, knowing he would take a bullet, a knife, his own life to see the Zanetti family thrive.

From the time she took her first steps, to her first word, all of it, Maxwell had been a proud daddy.

Alonzo released her hand as they got to the library, and he took a seat on one of the long sofas.

"Sit down," he said.

She sat on the edge of the sofa.

Tense.

Unyielding.

Petrified.

He didn't want her to be scared.

At thirty-five years old, he'd never felt anything for a woman other than the most basic need. With Tessa, it was different. The moment he told her about her parents' death, he watched her fall apart. She screamed, cried, sobbed, and seeing that kind of emotion and love, it had torn at his heart.

A heart he didn't think he had.

Her hands rested on her knees, and she wasn't looking at him. He wanted her to look at him.

"You're not supposed to be doing all the work with Caesar."

She lifted her head.

Success.

"I'm his nanny."

"Last time I checked I employed two of them. I'm not ignorant of the fact Michele likes to do anything but what I tell her to, unless she thinks she looks good. But I don't have time to employ another nanny, especially one that will keep her mouth shut. You shouldn't be doing everything."

"I love looking after him. He's a sweet boy."

"He's not going to stay sweet very long." He had no choice but to remind her. He was Zanetti and Adesso blood. He would become a made man, a member of their mafia world, and because of that, he would have no choice but to make hard decisions. There would be no getting out of this world for him. "If you continue to mother him, he will not adapt well."

"Why does it have to be this way? Why can't your children take over?"

Staring at Tessa, he had an overwhelming feeling to see her heavily pregnant with his child, her virgin body belonging to him.

To have her look at him with an even deeper love and adoration than she once had for her parents. He'd never experienced that kind of emotion.

"Were you not loved by your mother?" she asked.

"No," he said. "She knew what I was to become and gave all that love and devotion to Jessica. You ever wonder why she's a spoiled little bitch, thank our mother. She made her that way. Whatever she wanted, she got. I was taught how to be hard. How to kill a man. By the time I was fifteen I'd already killed five men. There's no room for softness in a man like me, Tessa."

He saw tears fill her eyes. "Then I feel sorry for you."

"You shouldn't feel sorry for me at all." He stared down her body. No matter how much she tried to hide them, her tits were like a beacon. He'd watched her for two years sneaking out of every single room that he entered.

She didn't think anyone noticed her.

He did.

Every time he watched her leave a room it had always been on the tip of his tongue to make her stay because he knew he could. Being one of the most feared men in the world helped with that.

Tessa feared him. He saw it in the way her eyes would often go wide when he entered a room. Her hands always shook as well.

There's no way he'd hurt her though.

Not after he heard the pain in her voice at losing her father.

He was many things, but hurting *her* like that, he couldn't do.

"I'm sorry," she said.

He smiled. "You don't need to be sorry either."

"I don't understand what you want."

"I want you to relax."

"Mr. Zanetti, I work for you."

"Call me Alonzo."

"I can't," she said.

"Why not?"

"That's disrespectful."

"Only if I demand you call me that and you insist on not. I wish for you to call me Alonzo."

He watched her teeth sink into her bottom lip. He'd give anything to taste her sweet lips. They looked so soft, so inviting.

His cock started to stir as he imagined those lips wrapped around it, taking him to the back of her throat.

She was a good girl. Two years without leaving his home, and before then, her father would always brag about her being a special girl.

He wanted a taste.

Craved her in ways he really shouldn't.

He wasn't a good man.

He wanted to make her dirty, to fuck her raw, and to make her beg. When it came to Tessa, it seemed his … obsession knew no bounds. He had her followed everywhere she went, not just for her own safety, for himself. There was also a guard at the house who he employed just for her.

Again, she didn't know it, and few of his men were aware of it.

He didn't allow everyone to know his business.

Tessa wasn't just some random whore he liked to use. She meant more to him, and he wouldn't dream of putting her life in danger.

"Come on, Tessa, give it a try. Let me hear my name from your lips."

He hoped she'd argue. Instead, she took a deep breath and said his name so softly that at first he didn't think he heard it.

"Again," he said.

"Alonzo."

Damn. Her voice sounded so good. He'd gladly listen to her all day long.

"That wasn't so bad, was it?"

She shook her head.

"Good, from now on, at the end of the day, I want you to come here."

"What?" she asked, the frown back in full force.

"You heard me."

"I don't understand what I've done wrong, sir."

"I like that coming from your lips." He winked at her. "You've done nothing wrong, but at the end of each day, I want you here so I can see you. I want to know what you're doing and how your day has gone."

"Is this what you do with Michele?" she asked, with no hint of jealousy in her voice.

"No, this is something special for you."

Chapter Two

The following day, after tucking Caesar into bed, Tessa put the baby monitor in her pocket and debated if she should just go to her room. She didn't live in any of the large wings in the house. There was part of the house in the back that was a lot smaller, for the people Alonzo employed who stayed on overnight to sleep.

She loved her room for a lot of reasons, and right now, she would give anything to go back there.

Alonzo wasn't known for his patience, and she worried if she pushed him too hard, he'd push back and it would end up hurting a lot more for her, and she was afraid of that.

Nibbling her lip, she tried not to think about everything bad that could happen to her, and just walked toward the library. The door was closed. She couldn't just walk into the room.

As she raised her fist, all of her survival instincts were telling her to run, to get the hell out of there.

Instead, she knocked and waited.

"Come in," he said.

She wished he'd not been there.

Opening the door, she stepped inside.

He sat on the same sofa, a glass of whiskey in his hand, as that was the only drink he ever had, and paperwork on his knee.

"I thought I'd have to send either Cole or Demetri to find you," he said.

"You told me to come, and I didn't get a notice that you changed your mind." She didn't exactly need to tell him the obvious, but she didn't have anything else to say.

"Take a seat. What would you like? Whiskey? Wine? Coffee? Tea? Hot chocolate?"

"Erm, hot chocolate please."

He chuckled. "I figured." He got up from his seat, and she watched him walk toward the desk. "Yes, bring that hot chocolate order now, please. Marshmallows?" Alonzo asked.

"Huh?"

"Do you want marshmallows?"

"Oh, no, that's fine. I don't like them."

He gave the order and put the phone down. "Who doesn't like marshmallows?"

"Me," she said, offering him a smile.

This was so incredibly hard. She wanted to hide. To be anywhere else but staring at him. Glancing around the library, she wondered what topics she could talk about that were relatively safe.

"I happen to like them. Especially near a bonfire. I love toasting them," Alonzo said.

"You do?"

"Yep. I love them hot and sticky. The best things in life are … worth waiting for."

Silence fell between them, and she didn't have a clue as to what he was referring to. This was all in the dark for her.

"Why do you have the baby monitor?" he asked, nodding at her jeans.

The top of the monitor was peeking out of her pocket.

"It's a force of habit. I put him to bed, and it's my responsibility."

"You do know some stuff is for the parents to do."

"Mr. and Mrs. Adesso are not home tonight."

"They're not?" he asked.

"They left a few hours ago."

Alonzo sat back, cursing. "They have no regard

for that boy."

"I'm his nanny. It's fine."

"You're not his mommy though, Tessa. Your life is not supposed to be wrapped up in a one-year-old child."

"If I'm not his nanny then what else do I do? I've got nowhere to go, and I was told to remain here, I had to work. I adore Caesar. He's a wonderful child."

"You love children?" he asked.

She smiled. "That's a leap. I adore Caesar. I don't know if I love every single child I meet. I've been out shopping with him and there are a couple of kids that are not at all friendly, but I like to think he is or at least he'll remain that way for a little while."

"Referring to the fact that everyone else within the mafia is not nice?"

Tessa felt sick to her stomach.

This man could kill her. Have her tortured for days and leave her to bleed out so the rats would feed on her flesh. Running her hands up her arms, she tried not to show her nerves.

"My dad always told me that the most feared men worked for the mafia. That you all had to do bad things." It was kind of immature, looking back at it. She'd been young, maybe ten or twelve, when she asked her father about his job.

There were a lot of things he must have done for the men he worked for.

"Tell me, Tessa, have you ever considered going to the cops?" he asked.

"You're in by blood. There's no out, Tessa. Never."

"But ... why don't you tell the cops?"

"I'll never rat. Those men, they may not see me as family, but they are mine. I will protect them with my

life because if anything happens to me, I know you and your mother will always, always be taken care of."

She'd stumbled onto her father taking care of some of his wounds. He'd been slashed with a knife. His complete devotion to these men had terrified her, but looking back, he was a loyal man.

Someone to admire, no matter who he worked for.

She was proud to have been his daughter.

"I'd never be a rat. My father had a strong belief, and I would never hurt his memory by turning on those he considered his family."

"Even if you hate us?" Alonzo asked.

"I don't hate you."

"You always run and hide," he said.

She frowned. "I was told that being a nanny meant I couldn't be seen or heard. No one wanted a screaming kid, and no one wanted a besotted nanny."

"Do you think you could be besotted?"

"I have no idea what you're talking about."

"I know, and it's refreshing."

There was a knock at the door, and she was thankful for the reprieve. She couldn't handle another second right now. Conversations with Alonzo hadn't exactly been on her list of things to deal with.

This was … weird.

In a good way though.

She rather liked his smile. He didn't do it enough, that was for sure. When he got older, he'd probably have a lot more frown lines than those that showed a lifetime of happiness.

Locking her fingers together, she watched as Cole entered the room. He was one of Alonzo's bodyguards. He held a large mug of chocolate, no marshmallows in sight.

"Thank you," she said, as he placed the mug down on the table.

"You're most welcome. Sir." He turned on his heel and left.

"One hot chocolate for you," Alonzo said.

"Do you get everyone in your employ to do your bidding?"

"I'm a Zanetti. If I wanted him to walk over broken glass, he would."

"Do you often make suggestions like that?"

"Why? Are you worried?"

"I don't imagine it inspires a great deal of loyal following if you act ... mean to them." She was going to say "like a dick," but thought better of it.

Just because they were enjoying a drink together didn't mean she could see him as a friend.

"You'd be surprised how I get my loyal following."

She chuckled. "You make them sound like a group of girls and you're the jock."

This he did smile at again. She liked it a lot and wanted to see him doing it more often.

"You know Michele would love a private meeting with you," she said.

Instantly, the smile was gone.

"Michele will not get a single meeting with me. Private or otherwise."

"I think she has a crush."

"Women that have crushes don't go spreading their legs for every single dick that looks to sink it into a hole."

Her cheeks heated. She'd never been spoken to like that before.

Michele was known for talking blatantly, and when men came to her, they always had something dirty to say to her.

Tessa was still a virgin at twenty years old and wasn't about to sleep with some random guy to get rid of it. She wanted her first time to be special.

When her mother was alive, she'd actually talked to her about it. Her mother had thought it had to be special for a young woman's first time, and there was no shame in wanting that either.

"Have I offended you?" Alonzo asked.

"Of course not."

Hearing the dirty talk from his lips had shocked her a little, and what was more, she rather liked that he didn't hold back.

Lifting up the mug of hot chocolate, she blew on the surface of the steaming mug, and took a sip.

It was delicious as she had no doubt it would be.

****

For the next week, each of their meetings was the same dance. Alonzo would be sitting there, waiting. Tessa would knock, and he noticed on days she really didn't want to be near him, she'd only knock lightly.

He'd be listening for it though.

If she thought she was going to get out of this easily, she had another think coming.

Out of all of his life, the only part of his day he enjoyed so much was having her close to him.

Of course, it didn't end the way he hoped either.

Tessa was never all over him, laughing at his jokes. She didn't wear clothes to lure him in or say suggestive things. Whenever he did talk dirty, her cheeks would go a beautiful shade of pink that made him think about taking her in front of a mirror, to see if her entire body would blush at the things he wanted to do to her.

He had no doubt at all that her father wouldn't have been happy with their union. Maxwell had been clear that he wanted his daughter to have a choice, a life away from the mafia.

Alonzo did have good intentions at the beginning, but like all good things, he'd discovered it was easier said than done.

He liked having her around his home, hearing her voice as she spoke softly to Caesar. The men, the guards, they respected her, and treated her with kindness.

Anyone who ever raised their voice to her had been dealt with by him. When she first moved to his home after her parents' passing, one of the guards had shoved her hard after telling her she was fat and useless. The encounter had been brought to his awareness, and he'd seen the evidence of it on his security footage. That man was no longer working for him.

Rubbing the back of his neck, he poured himself another generous amount of whiskey and waited.

She always put Caesar to bed.

He had a camera in the nursery, and with a few taps on his cell phone, he brought up the feed. She stood beside the crib.

Caesar was getting too big for it and would soon need a bed.

It pissed him off that neither Jessica nor Benedict were anywhere in sight. Neither was Michele.

He didn't go looking for her. Her lips were probably wrapped around a man's cock right now. She had tried to gain his attention many times. Alonzo had no interest in her.

The only woman he wanted was right there in the nursery, caring for a child that was not her own. Her beautiful voice sang a tune to Caesar as the young boy fell asleep.

She would be a good mother one day. He had no doubt. Tessa was a nice woman, sweet and kind.

There was a knock at the door.

Gritting his teeth, he closed the screen and called for whoever it was to enter. They did so at risk of inciting his wrath. He wasn't in a good mood whenever his stalking was interrupted.

"What is it?" he asked, calling out.

Seconds later, Cole entered his library, looking pissed.

"Why do I have a feeling I'm not going to like what you're about to tell me?"

"Louis's restaurant was just attacked. Rumor has it the cartels paid for the hit," Cole said.

Running a hand down his face, he didn't need to hear this shit. "We don't have any beef with the cartels. That makes no sense."

"Agreed, but that doesn't mean they don't want more territory. They want more of the drug business, and we don't use them as our supplier. Any deal they make you take a percentage of. I also heard their leader was shot and killed three weeks ago."

Standing up, Alonzo finished off his whiskey and didn't like that he was about to spend the rest of his night dealing with a fucking attack that wasn't planned, and they didn't stop. They were the Zanetti mafia. They controlled the city, and people paid them handsomely to keep them safe.

This wasn't good, and it was only just beginning.

There was a knock as there always was.

"Sir?" Cole asked.

His men knew he asked for Tessa to join him at the end of a day. He'd been dealing with strip clubs, the drugs, and the guns today. He was also having to deal with Adesso. His brother-in-law wanted to start getting a hand in trafficking women.

He didn't deal with trafficking humans of any

kind.

Yes, there was a fortune to be made in human flesh, but it was something that he viewed only with disgust. Watching men, women, and children being auctioned away as either easy labor or sex slaves didn't appeal to him.

Not that he didn't have whores.

The Zanettis owned several brothels and dealt in pussy, but those women knew the score. Like all things, he took his cut.

His own father hadn't respected the whole industry, regardless of how much it earned. Still, he knew what he was doing.

"Where is Adesso?" he asked. He certainly hadn't been tucking in his son.

He still didn't understand why his father on his deathbed wished for Jessica to marry the son of a bitch. It wasn't like she was happy or had even begged for a husband.

Jessica, his poor sister, had wanted to marry for love.

His mother on the other hand, had been pissed off that her husband had given their daughter away as his last wish.

"Come in," he said.

Tessa appeared a second later. The moment she caught sight of Cole, she stopped.

"What do you want me to do?" Cole asked.

"Find Adesso. I have a feeling his meddling caused this, and bring the car around. We're going to pay Louis a visit."

Cole nodded, turned on his heel, and left.

"Is everything okay?" she asked.

"Everything will be okay. I've got to cut our night short, I'm afraid."

He didn't like how happy she looked at that idea.

"You're off tomorrow. We're going out."

"Excuse me?"

"I'd like to take you shopping." Surely that would appeal.

"Shopping?"

"Am I not speaking clear English?" he asked.

"I just, I don't understand."

"Simple. You don't take enough vacation time. I employ two nannies for my sister, not just one. You will spend tomorrow with me. We're going to get you some new clothes." The ones he always caught her in looked old. She didn't even spend any of the money he paid her.

He knew this for a fact because he checked her bank account. Nothing was spent. She didn't need to buy any personal toiletries or food as it all came from him anyway. There was nothing she could ever want as he took care of it all.

Now though, he was determined for her to have fun. He'd given her time to grieve, to deal with the loss of her parents. He was done waiting around.

Done being patient.

He wasn't known for taking no for an answer.

Tessa was his.

She didn't know it yet, but she would.

"You really don't need to do that though. I don't understand why you would."

"Simple, I want to spend time with you. To do that, I have to be with you." He stepped up close to her. She tensed but didn't step back.

Progress.

He expected her to turn on her heel and run.

No, Tessa was a fighter.

"I have to go now," he said, reaching out, cupping her cheek. She didn't accept his touch easily.

One day, he would have her craving his touch. When he put his mind to something that he wanted, he wouldn't stop until he got it.

Tessa, owning her, she'd be a sweet victory.

With his father dead, he didn't have anyone to dictate to him who he'd be with. Tessa wasn't family nor mafia royalty, but he wasn't going to be told who he could marry.

She belonged to him. He'd known it for some time now, maybe even before she became a nanny.

Stroking his thumb across her bottom lip, he watched her gasp. He wanted nothing more than to take her lips, but then he'd have to leave.

When he finally kissed her, there wasn't going to be time for him to go anywhere. He wanted the time to explore her body, to take, to touch, to taste.

His cock hardened at the thought of her body beneath his, her virgin pussy spreading for no one else but him.

"I hope you enjoy your hot chocolate and think about me tonight, Tessa." He leaned in close, tempted to kiss her.

No, he couldn't do it.

Pulling away, he stepped back and left the library. When he started, he wasn't going to stop.

Chapter Three

Tessa finished changing Caesar's diaper. She wrapped up the old one, placing it in the trash bin in the corner and washing her hands. Once that was done, she started to dress Caesar. She knew she had to get ready for her day out with Alonzo, but no one had responded to Caesar's cries. She could only take so much, so she didn't have much choice but to come and take care of him.

"There, there, all better now. You really know how to poop through the night, don't you?" She kissed Caesar's head and sighed. He was such a good boy.

He started to play with her necklace, and she smiled at him, letting him do that. With him in her arms, she sat down with him in the rocking chair. If no one came to relieve her of him in the next ten minutes, she'd take him down to feed him.

She loved her job and taking care of Caesar, but now her thoughts kept going to Alonzo and why he demanded she spend some time with him. It made no sense to her, none at all.

In fact, she found the entire thing stressful.

When Caesar started to make a fuss, she knew she had to feed him.

"Come on, little guy. Let's take you downstairs and get some food." She placed him on her hip. He was so happy when she did that, as her hips were quite large, and he settled in so nicely.

Humming to herself, she walked downstairs to the kitchen.

Louise, the cook, wasn't even there when she entered the kitchen. Pulling the high chair to the counter, she grabbed Caesar's food, which Louise always made in advance for him. It was something mashed together.

He didn't like a lot of the mushed-up foods. If he didn't eat this porridge-looking stuff, she'd mash him up a banana to eat.

She took a seat next to him and started to do the helicopter noises. The moment the food hit his taste buds, he gave her that horrible baby look and proceeded to spit it out.

"Oh, no, is that really nasty? It looks really bad, and I shouldn't be saying that. I'm an awful person."

She took a small taste and scrunched up her own nose. "Don't you worry. One day you'll be able to have fried chicken, meatballs, ice cream, and I love cookies so, so much. I also love putting ice cream between cookies, and that is even better. This though, is nasty."

"You shouldn't be encouraging him to not eat that," Alonzo said.

She jerked up in her seat, taken aback by his sudden appearance.

"Alonzo," she said.

"I was waiting for you in the library."

"I'm really sorry. I … I had to take care of Caesar."

"I told you today was your day off."

"No one attended to him. I did wait. You know, I did wait. I remembered." She pointed at the clothes she wore. "I got changed." Realizing one of her stained shirts covered the evidence that she had changed to go out, she quickly tugged it off. Her cheeks heated when the shirt rode up, and she had this horrible feeling she'd just shown her boss her bra. "See, I had changed."

"And no one responded to Caesar's cries."

"I did wait a few minutes."

"I understand." He already turned his back on her and was pressing buttons on his cell phone.

"I hope I didn't get anyone in trouble," she said,

talking to her charge.

Caesar slapped his hands, and she grabbed a banana, a small bowl, and another spoon. She mashed it up so there were also a few chunks.

"Wait until you can have peanut butter. That stuff is deadly. Honestly, it will go straight to your hips, but it will be so worth it." She winked at Caesar as she fed him.

She didn't know what Alonzo said, but Jessica was the first to enter the room. She looked awful.

Her hair was all matted as if she'd just passed out with hair gel in it.

"I can't believe you woke me up to take care of my kid. Tessa is doing a perfectly good job of it."

"He's your son, Jessica," Alonzo said.

Tessa watched as he stepped back into the room. She hated all kinds of conflict, and seeing these two argue always unnerved her.

Jessica, for the most part, was nice.

"So! I don't see you getting Benedict here to deal with him. Just because I'm a woman doesn't mean I have to feed him. I've got a life as well." Jessica let out a cry as she was pulled out of the room.

They hadn't gone far, and Tessa heard everything that was said between the two.

"Right now, you are a fucking embarrassment to me and to this family."

"Why employ nannies if we're not going to use them? Tessa is damn good at what she does and you know it."

"Because I'm taking her out, and I told you this last night."

Silence met his answer.

"Oh," Jessica said.

"Yes, oh. Now take over feeding your son. Start

looking for a new nanny in order to replace Tessa when the need is there. I don't want him going without because of me."

They both entered, and Tessa quickly scooped up some banana and fed it to a waiting Caesar.

"Tessa, my office now. We're having breakfast before we go."

"I don't mind—"

"Now!"

She quickly passed the bowl to Jessica and followed behind Alonzo.

He didn't take no for an answer and she hated being yelled at, so she followed him. It was hard not to burst into tears, but by the time she got to his office, she had her emotions under control.

His office always reminded her of something out of the fifties. The shelves were laden with books that didn't look used. The desk, wooden and large, filled most of the space in front of the window with a large leather chair behind it.

Alonzo didn't go toward the chair though.

There was a small coffee table in front of two sofas. Taking a seat that Alonzo pointed out, she stared at the food. Lots of different fruits were out on the table, along with toasts, jams, and spreads. There were some mini boxes of cereal as well, which she found so utterly cute.

"Take what you like."

"There's a lot here to choose from."

Alonzo had already taken a slice of toast and spread some jam over it thickly. Picking up a piece of orange, she took a bite, moaning as the sweet fruit filled her mouth. The taste was amazing. She normally had a couple of slices of toast for breakfast.

Neither of them spoke as Alonzo poured them

both some coffee. She accepted hers black. Every now and then she found herself drawn to him as he read the newspaper.

"Did everything go okay last night?" She'd been worried about him.

"As well as could be expected. Tell me, Tessa, did you miss me?"

"I was worried about you."

"You were?"

"Yes."

"I don't suppose you happen to enjoy our time together?"

Biting her lip, she couldn't look away. His gaze held her locked in place with no way of escaping.

"I ... do." He made her afraid at times, but she'd come to enjoy listening to him talk, answering his never-ending questions. She loved seeing him smile. He didn't do it often enough.

There were times he reminded her of her father. He'd spent a great deal of time sad, alone, miserable.

This kind of work couldn't have been easy.

She wasn't under any illusions about the kind of work he did or what the mafia were. It was a kill-or-be-killed world out there. When she learned the truth, she'd found it hard to deal, to think of her father as a killer.

Her mother had told her that there was so much bad stuff going on in this world. She couldn't help the man she fell in love with, but she wasn't going to hold his life against him. If given the choice between her husband killing or being killed, she would have him do the killing.

Tessa glanced at Alonzo, who stared back at her.

Would she be able to handle him killing, anyone killing?

Pushing those thoughts to the back of her mind,

she offered him a smile.

"You look petrified."

"Shopping is not something I've ever enjoyed."

"Now this is a new experience for me. I've never met a woman who hasn't enjoyed spending my money."

"Oh, I don't want to spend your money."

"I wouldn't expect you to spend your own, Tessa. Now, come. I intend to get you out of this house. You've been looking way too pale lately."

****

The mall was the last place Alonzo wanted to be. However, he wished to spoil Tessa and to do it with her. They'd already entered five designer shops, and none of them held any appeal to her. She'd walked through the rows, looking at shirts or jeans. None of the dresses had even been glanced at.

When she saw the price tag, she'd drop it and move on to the next one.

By the time lunch came around, he sat at the table with Cole and Demetri. Tessa had excused herself to use the bathroom. She begged to go alone, and he didn't see a problem with it. He'd never been this stuck with women, not during his entire adult life.

"You know, you could pick out clothes for her," Cole said.

"I don't need your advice."

"Clearly, you do. We get that to the outside world we're not your friends. We're your guards. Come on, we know what Tessa means to you. She's also being really difficult and stubborn," Demetri said.

"I don't think she's stubborn," Cole said. He took a long sip of his milkshake. "I don't think she's used to having this kind of attention. I remember her dad. He hated going shopping with her because he'd always moan about how she was a pain in the ass. More of a boy than a girl." Cole laughed. "Honestly, he'd rather face twenty-four hours of torture than take her shopping."

"Be your Alonzo pain in the ass self," Demetri said. "Don't give her time to say no. Just do."

He couldn't believe he was taking advice from his friends. Cole and Demetri had awful taste in women, mainly because they only ever fucked whores.

"Fine, fine."

Tessa left the bathroom, taking a seat.

"Have you called Jessica?" she asked.

"Why would I call her? She's not my keeper."

"To see how Caesar's doing. It's his lunchtime, and he doesn't like the sweet potato that Louise does for him."

"Does he like anything Louise cooks for him?" Alonzo asked.

"Not really, but he's going through that phase where he likes something and then doesn't. It's a thing."

"He's not even a teenager, and he has a thing."

She shrugged.

"Get lost," he said to his men.

Cole and Demetri grabbed their food and walked three tables down, dropping down into the chairs.

"You can't just do that."

"Do what?"

"Order them to leave. That was so rude."

"First of all, they're here to keep me safe. Second, I'm here with you, and you keep looking at their guns."

"Do they really need them in public? It could scare the kids." She didn't ask in a judgmental tone.

He noticed that. She never told or asked or gossiped. She just seemed to exist.

Since he'd told her about her parents, something had broken inside her, and he was determined to fix it, to make her find that fire and passion again.

"I could be killed at any second."

Tessa looked around. "We should have stayed home. You didn't have to put your life in danger for me. Believe me, it's not worth it."

That just pissed him off. As far as he was concerned, she was worth it without a doubt.

"My life has been threatened since I was a young boy. That's not going to change."

"Doesn't that bother you?" she asked. "That people want to kill you?"

"No. I can deal with everything they have to throw at me."

"I don't think I could handle that. People wanting to kill me. I struggle when they yell at me." She rolled her eyes.

"You don't like people yelling at you?"

"I don't even know why I told you that, but yes, I don't like it when it happens. Teachers were the worst about it, and it was so embarrassing."

"You know any teachers that were mean to you I can deal with."

She burst out laughing. "I don't want anyone's blood on my hands." She winced. "I don't mean to insult what you do or anything. I'm just, I don't like violence of any kind, and I'm really not good with all of this. I'm so sorry."

"You've got nothing to apologize for." He didn't find her insulting.

It was a simple fact. He was dangerous, and she wasn't.

They finished up their lunch, and he took her hand.

Cole and Demetri kept their distance, and he was always vigilant. This was a stupid thing for him to do, but he hoped by not planning it there was no risk of his whereabouts getting out.

Besides, he was in a very public place, and any shootout would bring media attention. None of them wanted that as it brought heat to all of them, and anyone who was willing to risk that kind of exposure wouldn't last very long.

He walked into one of the shops. Tessa went off in her own direction, and instead of following her around, he started to look at the clothes himself.

Seeing a few items he wanted her to try on, he walked up to Tessa. "Don't mind me." He tugged on her jeans as she let out a little cry. "You don't want to draw attention to us. If I was you, I'd stay perfectly quiet."

"What are you doing?"

He saw her size and moved to her shirt, finding the tag at the bottom. "Excellent, follow me." He took her hand, taking charge of their shopping experience. Even as she protested, he found some dresses and skirts. He was tired of seeing her in jeans and large shirts.

Once he had several items picked out, he pulled her toward the changing room.

"You can't do this."

"Guess again, Tessa. I can do whatever I want. Today was about bringing you out and seeing you try on some new clothes. Now I get to see every single item."

"You're kidding?" she asked.

He took a seat in the plush chair. "Not at all. If I don't see everything I've given you, I'm coming in there to take over. If you want to test me, go ahead. I'll gladly get you naked."

"I don't know what this is," she said. "You're my boss. I'm confused."

"Technically, my sister is your boss."

She frowned. "But you pay my wages."

"Stop thinking. Enjoy and go and put the damn clothes on. I want to see everything."

He leaned back in his chair, watching her ass for the few seconds he saw it sway. She didn't linger and pulled the curtain back into place. He saw a couple of women checking him out, but he had no use for them.

The only one he wanted was the stubborn young woman behind the curtain.

She opened it back up as she modeled a knee-length black skirt and sexy-as-fuck blouse. He could imagine fucking her across the table in the library.

"Good."

She rolled her eyes. The curtain closed again, and he stared at the floor. Her ankles were visible. She wore a pair of sports socks that fit to her ankles. The skirt dropped to the floor, and he wondered if he could get away with making her change into some new lingerie.

No, it was too early. He didn't want to push her too far.

She opened the curtain, and he accepted the outfits. Some were just to screw with her, while others were for places he hoped to take her.

After twenty minutes, she finally called his name.

"What is it?"

"Will you come here, please?" she asked.

Getting to his feet, he pocketed his cell phone and opened the curtain. In the mirror he saw the long expanse of her back. "I need you to help me zip it up if that's okay. I don't know if it's the right size."

The dress she had on was red, and he'd picked it with the intention of taking her out one night on the town.

Stepping behind the curtain, he made sure it was closed.

"Let me," he said.

She kept nibbling that lip of hers even as she turned, giving him her back.

She wore a plain white bra. He couldn't resist touching the strap.

"What are you doing?" she asked.

Gripping the zipper, he held the dress together and slowly slid it up, making sure he touched as much of her skin as possible without it seeming too obvious.

She let out a gasp as he put a hand to her hip afterward. Staring at her reflection, he breathed against her neck. Her nipples stood out, and as he teased her hip, he watched as they got tighter.

Her eyes dilated, and she looked so good.

He wanted to fuck her there. Instead, he cupped her ass. "This fits you really well."

"I can't accept this. It would be a waste of money."

"Why?"

"I've got nowhere to go out in it. It would be silly to have it."

"I want you to have it."

"We can't always have what we want," she said.

"I can."

Chapter Four

After a busy morning of walking Caesar around the garden and letting him enjoy some time on the grass, Tessa had brought him back to the nursery and put him down for a nap. Michele was nowhere to be found, and the last she saw of Jessica, she was arguing with Benedict.

Yesterday's shopping trip with Alonzo had been … interesting. She didn't know what else to think about the time she spent with him. He'd made her purchase all of the clothes he'd picked out, including the red evening dress she had every intention of returning. They packages were due to be delivered by the end of the week.

She didn't know what to think of his sudden interest in her. It wasn't like she encouraged him to like her.

"I'm overthinking it. I know I am."

She hadn't seen him that morning. She didn't know if she should still visit him tonight or not. He made everything so confusing to her.

Rubbing the back of her neck, she reached down, picking up Caesar's used clothing. She'd changed him in such a hurry. He was constantly trying to scurry away, and even though he wanted to fall asleep, he still made her work for it.

She was folding the previous day's washing and putting it away when the door opened silently.

She saw Jessica enter, her head pressed against the door.

Seconds later, she heard a sob.

At first Tessa didn't have a clue what to do. This wasn't part of her job description, and even though she worked for Jessica, they didn't exactly get along. Neither of them really spoke about anything.

Jessica never had any input about her baby.

When another sob echoed around the room, she was worried it would wake Caesar up, and then it would be a nightmare to get him back to sleep. He became really cranky if his sleep was interrupted.

"Are you okay?" she asked.

Jessica gave a tiny gasp and whirled around. "You? What the hell are you doing here?"

"It's Caesar's naptime. I put him down for a nap."

Jessica put her fingers to her lips, and tears filled her eyes. "Oh, yes, of course. Yes, it's Caesar's naptime."

When she moved her hands, Tessa saw the blood coming from her nose.

"What happened?"

"What?" Jessica asked.

"Your nose."

She touched her nose coming away with blood on her fingertips. "It's nothing."

"That doesn't look like nothing." She hated to see her in pain.

"I deserved it. I shouldn't ask questions. This is entirely my fault."

"I don't believe that. Would it be okay if I helped clean you up?"

"Yes, of course. You don't have to though."

Taking Jessica's hands, she led her into the bathroom. As she made her take a seat on the toilet, guilt filled Tessa. She'd never seen Benedict hit Jessica. She'd heard the sounds but never saw it.

Her father always told her to stay out of other people's business. Moments like this, she had to wonder how her father did it. How he was able to stay out of someone's business who was clearly being hurt.

Filling the pristine white sink with warm water,

she grabbed one of the fluffiest towels there was.

There seemed to be a fascination with the purest of white. She wondered if this had something to do with the fact they were all far from pure.

Dipping the towel into the water, she got it nice and wet.

"Have you told your brother?" she asked.

"He wouldn't do anything about it."

"You don't know that," Tessa said.

"He thinks I deserve it."

"No woman deserves to get hit." She started to press the cloth against the blood, wiping it away. More bruising had come out. She also wiped away a thick layer of makeup. It had to be the way she was hiding it from Alonzo. She didn't want to think of him as ignoring his sister's pain.

It doesn't matter what he does.

He can do whatever he wants.

You're nothing.

"Did you enjoy your shopping trip?" Jessica asked.

"It was okay."

"You don't sound happy about it. I know my brother can be a pain in the ass."

"I don't like shopping."

Jessica snorted. "Please, we all love shopping."

"Then I must be weird because I never enjoyed it. Not even growing up at home. I hated it when it came time for it."

"You're right. It's weird. Shopping is something I'm an expert at. I could gladly do it all day every single day."

"Are you happy?" Tessa asked.

"I'm sorry?"

"Forget it. I shouldn't have asked. It was stupid of

me."

"You want to know if I'm happy."

"It doesn't matter. I'm so stupid for asking. Honestly, it's not my place."

She wiped some more of the blood away, wishing she had a filter to stop herself from asking stupid questions.

"No, I'm not happy," Jessica said. "You know, you're the first person to ask me."

"I am?"

"Yes. In our world, no one cares about the women. We're a means to an end. Because we don't have a dick, we're expendable. Men use us for their own personal pleasure. I envy normal girls. Women that didn't start out as a Zanetti."

"You don't love your husband?"

"I hate him," Jessica said, snorting. "I didn't want to marry him. It was my dying father's wish to see me marry Benedict. If I could get away with it, I would shoot him. He's out screwing everyone and everything. I don't want him to touch me." Jessica looked into the nursery. "I ... I don't love him."

This made Tessa pause. She didn't want to say anything, not right now.

"I know that I sound horrible, but I ... I don't love him. I don't feel anything toward him. He's so cute. So small. So perfect and he was healthy. So many women can't have babies, and I had a healthy one. A good one." She sniffled. "It's just another trap. Something to keep me tied to Benedict, and I hate him even more. I know you don't want or need to hear this."

"I'm so sorry you feel that way."

"You care about him, don't you?"

"I think you need to talk to Alonzo."

"I won't hurt him," Jessica said. "I will never

harm that baby, but I won't ever love him. I don't have it in me to love a monster." Jessica took the towel from her hands. "If you are wise you will listen to me and you will find a way to get out. To get out and leave here. To never look back."

"Jessica?"

"I will take it from here. Go away," Jessica said.

Leaving the nursery, Tessa didn't know what to do. She truly believed Jessica wouldn't hurt Caesar, but she didn't know how to deal with the bruises, or the pain so clear in Jessica's eyes.

Seeing no other way to stop it, she walked to Alonzo's office. She didn't want to knock on the door, but she did.

"Who is it?" Alonzo asked. His voice sounded so threatening and scary.

"It's Tessa."

Seconds later the door opened. Alonzo's body covered the doorway.

"I'm so sorry. You're busy."

"What is it?" he asked.

"I wanted to talk to you about something."

"It can wait. Right now, I'm busy, and you need to go back to Caesar or elsewhere. I have business to deal with."

She didn't get a chance to say another word as he slammed the door closed.

Tears filled her eyes at how useless she felt.

Turning her back on the door, she started making her way back up to Caesar's room. The door was partially open, and as she went to open the door, she stopped. Jessica was in the rocking chair with a pillow around her body. She held Caesar in her arms.

The young boy was holding his mother's finger.

"Hello, sweet boy, you're not too bad, are you?

No. I bet you're spoiled. Tessa spoils you. I've watched her with you. She adores you, yes, she does. She'll be one hell of a mom one day. I'm not a good mother, Caesar. You're going to hate me because I can't bring myself to love you. The moment I knew you were a boy, I knew I couldn't have you. My mom warned me. She told me not to become attached to a son. A son didn't have a place with his mother. You're going to become an Adesso or a Zanetti. One day, I hope you can rule this place with an iron fist, but when you look at your wife, you're nothing but tender."

Stepping away from the door, Tessa walked back to her room.

Jessica may not want to love her son, but from what she heard, she already did.

****

Alonzo hadn't meant to be harsh with Tessa. He'd not expected her to come knocking on his office door when he was on a live call with the leader of the cartel. Neither of them wanted to meet in person, not with the rumors running rife that they'd attacked Louis's place.

Now, if he listened to all the families, they would have him attack. There was no way they would meet as it would only end in bloodshed. He had no interest in putting anyone's life in danger, regardless if his fellow family bosses wished for him to attack. He wasn't a fool, and he didn't crave unnecessary bloodshed, nor would he.

Sitting in the library, he saw he'd been waiting for Tessa for over an hour. He didn't know if she was being stubborn for how he sent her off or what.

He didn't have the head for this, not today.

Getting to his feet, he drank the last of his whiskey and walked straight to her room. He didn't care if anyone saw him.

He and Tessa had an agreement.

"Tessa, open the damn door," he said, slamming his fist against it. He wasn't above kicking her door open.

There were plenty of rooms in the house for her to stay in.

Running a hand down his face, he was pissed off.

The new leader of the cartels wanted to give him the runaround, and he wasn't interested in price bidding for land. Not to mention Benedict had arranged a meeting with a fucking trafficker, which pissed him off.

"What do you want?" Tessa asked, opening the bedroom door before he could slam his fist against it again.

"Why are you not at the library?"

She wore a pair of pajamas, and damn it, she looked sexy as fuck. His cock stirred at the sight of her.

"Why should I be at the library? You think you can talk to someone like that and then for everything to be okay?"

He wouldn't talk to her with the door separating them. Pushing it open, he stepped inside and glared at her.

"What are you doing?" she asked, stepping back.

"I was talking to a guy today that would tear your fucking flesh from your bones. I don't want him to know about you or to get close to you. You're not my boss, Tessa. I gave you an instruction."

"My job description is nanny. Not even for your kids. You don't get to boss me around."

He reached out, grabbing her, slamming her against the door. He took hold of her hands, pressing them above her head. "Oh, yeah, and who is going to stop me, Tessa? I can do what I like, when I like. I wasn't going to put you in danger. Not after I've done everything I can to keep you out of it."

"I don't want to argue."

He stared down at her. Her chest heaved with each indrawn breath, the hard buds of her nipples pressing against the front of her shirt.

She was so close that all it would take was for him to cup her tit to feel her. He wondered if she wore any panties beneath her pajama shorts.

"You shouldn't be here," she said.

"This is my house."

She wasn't fighting him to get out. Her gaze was on him, on his lips. He saw the need in her eyes even as she tried to fight it. There was nothing to fight, nothing.

He leaned in close.

"What are you doing?" she asked.

He didn't tell her.

Taking her lips beneath his, he kissed her hard, her fingers locking with his as he deepened the kiss. Sliding his tongue between her sweet lips, he tasted her. She stroked her tongue against his, and he released one of her hands to sink his fingers in her hair, to hold her against him.

She let out a whimper, and it was sheer fucking torture.

Pressing his cock against her stomach, he let her other hand go to grip her ass tightly, squeezing the plump flesh through the fabric of her pajamas.

This was exactly how he imagined her.

So perfect and right against his body.

She let out a sweet little gasp, and the sound drove him crazy. Running circles across her ass, he stroked down, cupping her knee to draw her leg over his hip. Rocking his cock against her pussy, he wanted nothing more than to tear their clothes off, to feel her riding his dick as he slid in deep.

There wouldn't be any condoms either. He wanted to feel her silken cunt wrapped around him.

Breaking from the kiss, he trailed his lips down her neck, sucking on her pulse.

"You ever been kissed before, Tessa?" He knew the truth but wanted to hear it from her lips first.

"No. We shouldn't be doing this."

"I can't think of anything else we should be doing." He lifted up her vest shirt, tugging it over her head, dropping it to the floor.

She didn't argue with him as he did this.

He saw her nerves, so he released her long enough to pull off his own shirt.

Her gaze landed on the ink that covered his chest and arms. He didn't have any problem with her looking her fill. Capturing her hips, he tugged her close, running his hands back over her curvy ass.

So ripe.

So full.

Soon, she'd be all his.

He'd intended to take his time, to seduce her, to make her fall.

Two years was a long enough wait for her. Now, he intended to have her, to fuck her, and to keep her.

Moving her back toward the bed, he pushed her down, capturing her pajama shorts. Tugging them off her body in one swift movement, he gripped her knees, spreading her thighs wide. "The next time we go shopping, I'm buying you lingerie. Sexy little pieces so I can think about your cute little pussy pressed against them."

The bra she wore had a catch in the front, and he flicked it open, her large tits spilling out. He noticed whenever she wore pajamas around the house, she always wore a bra beneath. He figured it was due to her large tits.

She went to hide her body from him, but he caught her hands. "No, you don't hide from me, not ever. I want to see you every single chance I get. You're perfection, Tessa. Don't ever think otherwise."

He cupped her tits, pressing them together. Teasing each hardened nipple, he skimmed the tips of his fingers down her body, going to her stomach then to her thighs. He knelt between them, and he touched her pussy, spreading her open so that he could see her slit.

She was already so wet. Touching her swollen clit, he teased across, over, and around her sweet nub.

"You're so wet, baby, so fucking perfect," he said. "You've never been touched before, have you?"

She shook her head.

"You ever given yourself an orgasm?" he asked.

She bit her lip again but nodded.

"You have? You touched this sweet little cunt."

"Yes."

"One day I'll get you to show me exactly what you do. I'd love to see you stroking yourself. I bet it's so fucking sexy."

He pinched her clit, seeing her cry out. Her body arched up off the bed, her tits shaking as he stroked her. She was … perfection.

"You ever think about me touching you?" he asked.

"No. You're my boss."

He took her clit between his lips and sucked hard. Releasing her, he stroked over her clit, going back and forth. "From now on, I want you to think about me. Think about my lips on your pussy. My cock sliding deep inside you, fucking you."

He gripped her ass, and lifting her pussy up

against his mouth, he started to lick and suck from her virgin cunt. So ripe, so ready for the taking.

He was going to ruin her for every other man, to have her come to him.

Lowering her down to the bed, he opened his pants, taking out his large dick. He was so hard, and the tip was leaking pre-cum already. Smearing his arousal into his length, he worked himself, moving up and down.

Licking her pussy, seeing her naked, spread out under him, was so right. This was why he'd been patient to begin with.

Tessa belonged to him, and he was going to keep her.

"I want you to come on my tongue, baby. Give it to me. Come for me."

She let out a whimper, and as he stroked over her clit, drawing her closer to the edge, he saw her body change, the way she started to tense up until she finally hurtled over the edge into bliss, crying his name. As it filled the air, he stroked her to orgasm, feeling his own start to build. His balls ached, and he wanted to shove himself deep inside her, but instead, he lifted up, taking possession of her lips as he came over her pussy and stomach.

There would be time to take her, to fill her with his cum.

That day wasn't today.

Chapter Five

After Alonzo made her come and he'd found his release on her stomach, he'd gone to her bathroom, grabbed a towel, cleaned his cum from her, and then left. It had to be one of the strangest, most erotic moments of her life.

Why had he left?

Did she do something wrong?

She'd brought herself to orgasm many times with her hands. She wasn't immune to wanting sex or even desiring it. There were times she wished a man would approach her, ask her out, or at least do something which would lead to sex. So far in her life, she'd gotten nothing, nada.

As far as her experiences went, last night failed on so many levels.

He licked her pussy, got his rocks off, and nothing else.

Didn't it lead to sex?

Did she even want sex?

Why the hell was she sitting in the library with Caesar crawling around, thinking about the man who'd gotten her off? He probably had a whole host of women crawling in and out of his bed, begging to be his plaything.

The last thing she wanted to do was to be his play anything.

She'd never even thought about Alonzo as anything other than her boss.

Now, it was like he'd crawled under her skin and she couldn't *stop* thinking about him. He was there all the time, and even as she smiled down at Caesar, who slapped her leg with one of his toys, Alonzo stayed there.

"Ah, I see you escaped here," Michele said,

entering the room.

Tessa looked up at the other nanny, who looked pissed off. "It's where we always go."

"And do what? Sit, watching him drool." Michele dropped down to the floor as if she was in trouble.

"Why did you take the job as a nanny if you can't stand kids?" she asked.

"Please, the pay is amazing. Besides, getting one of the made men or even a solider would be a step up in this world."

"That's what you're after, a guy?"

"Yep. I want to be taken care of. Working sucks. I don't want to scrub all my life for nothing at the end of it. If I've got to suck a bit of cock to get ahead in this world, I got no problem with that. Most women give it up for free. Me, I just want a little something at the end of it." Michele laughed. "Don't look so shocked, Tessa. Maybe you should spread those legs of yours and see what you can get. A virgin like you would get a pretty penny around here."

"No, thank you." She felt sick.

"You're too much of a prude. That's what Alonzo wants from you though. I bet he just wants to be the guy to get your cherry. To fuck you nice and hard and make you bleed as he does."

"Shut up," Tessa said.

"What are you going to do about it? I'm not going anywhere, Tessa. You think you can fuck the boss, get what you want. I'm not going to let you do that."

"You have no idea what the hell you're talking about." She got to her feet and started to pick up Caesar's toys.

"I know he came to your room last night. I heard the moans right outside your door. You act like you're all sweet and innocent, and you may be a virgin, but deep down, you're a slut. You're desperate for cock."

"I don't like the way you're talking in front of Caesar. Clean your mouth out or stop talking." She picked Caesar up.

"You better watch your step, Tessa. I know who you are, and you're going down."

Tessa's heart raced as she left the library. Caesar started to fidget in her arms, and she just needed to get out of the house.

Michele's words kept ringing inside her head, and no matter how hard she tried, she couldn't make them stop. She walked to the front of the house where one of the guards stood watch. His name was Liam, and she explained she wanted to take Caesar out. Within a matter of minutes, she had Caesar dressed and ready for a walk. Being his nanny, she had the responsibility of taking him out, feeding him, and knowing when to put him down for a nap, bathe him, everything.

She loved kids so much, and she hadn't even realized how much until she started to care for Caesar.

Even with Liam and another guard at her back, she drowned out their footsteps as they followed her.

They lived not too far from a park. It was a small one but offered a walkway for anyone who wanted to take some time away with a small play area for kids. She found it easier for her to think there.

Of course, it reminded her of the park where her parents always took her when she was growing up. She'd often sit on the swings with her father behind her, pushing her. He always told her to fly, to reach for the stars, to never let anything get her down.

Once inside the park, it was easier to drown out the two men. A couple of women gave her weird looks, but again, she ignored them. Pushing Caesar past the play area where a couple of kids were playing in the sand pit, she got onto the pathway and just started walking. This, to her, was better than any running machine. She got the fresh air and the feeling of actually going somewhere.

She didn't like Michele or her accusation, not one bit. She'd been working with the other woman for a year now, and there was just no getting past how … horrid the woman was.

Michele didn't care about Caesar. She only cared about herself, and it bugged her. Her accusations about her and Alonzo bothered her.

Last night wasn't supposed to happen, but it did. What the hell was she supposed to do now? How could she face him again?

This was all too much.

She'd have to quit.

With her father no longer part of his team, maybe she could live a quiet life. A life away from the mafia. Away from everything.

The thought alone filled her with such joy, and she couldn't contain her excitement and just being alone. Being herself.

With a spring in her step, she rounded the park four more times before finally heading toward the gate.

However, there was no chance of her escaping as the reason for her troubled thoughts stood right at the gate. She noticed all of the other parents and kids were gone. The park was completely empty.

Jessica stood at his side, as did Benedict.

"I didn't steal him," she said, walking faster so that she stood in front of them.

"We know you didn't, silly. We're here to take him. That's all."

Alonzo hadn't said a word.

"He should be ready for his feed," she said, handing over the stroller.

Jessica took it. "Thank you."

She watched as Jessica and Benedict both left. When he tried to put an arm around his wife, she pulled away. There really was no love there.

The two guards who'd followed her left to keep an eye on Jessica.

She stood alone with Alonzo, Cole, and Demetri.

"I don't like it when you leave the house without my permission," Alonzo said.

"I was only doing my job. I'm not allowed to do that anymore?" She looked past his shoulder, not liking others seeing her with him.

"Come," Alonzo said. He held out his hand, and she really didn't want to take it, but she did. They were in public, and this wouldn't go well for either of them if they got caught.

They walked toward the swings, and he ordered her to take a seat. Being ordered around started to grate on her nerves. Remembering the feel of his lips between her thighs though, she sat down on the seat.

His hand went to her back, and he gave her a gentle push. Rather than fight him, she lifted her legs up and allowed the push to carry her. When she drew her legs back, he pressed on her back, and she was once again in the air.

For a short time, she could imagine her father being here, or at least feel him in the air as she reached for the stars.

The longer she sat, climbing higher and higher, more of her troubles melted away until nothing was left. Nothing mattered in her life.

Not being a nanny.

Not Michele.

Not Alonzo.

Or the fear that her life would one day end in a

bloody war.

There simply was nothing.

****

It would have been so easy to fuck her last night. To take her cherry and have her screaming for him, begging for more. Only, Alonzo didn't just want her for sex. There was no way he'd waited two years for her for it all to be over in one night.

Clearly, she had trouble dealing with what they'd done together. He'd checked the surveillance footage he had around the house. From what he saw, she'd looked like a crazy person, needing to escape, and he didn't like it. He didn't like her wanting to get away from him.

He used Tessa's own momentum to watch her fly higher in the sky.

"What do you do on your downtime?" he asked, *looking at Maxwell. The older man was one of his most trusted allies and soldiers.*

"I take my daughter to the park."

"Isn't she a little old for the park?"

"Maybe. Either way, whatever troubles she has in her young mind, they melt away. All I have to do is give her a push."

The memory came to him fast, and as he pressed his hand against her back, watching her fly, he thought about her father. Maxwell had always been worried about her safety. About what being part of the mafia meant to her well-being.

This was not a place for everyone.

Even Alonzo had thought about leaving it behind, only he couldn't. Once he was part of it, there really was no going back.

Cole and Demetri stood away from them.

He checked the time, and saw it was a little after seven. They'd need to leave soon. She had to be hungry.

When she came back, he didn't push her again.

She started to slow down, and he moved to stand in front of her.

The smile died on her lips as she caught sight of him.

Slowly, back and forth, she stopped, and he stepped forward. When he gripped the chains of her swing, she stayed seated.

"Whenever you need to come out here to clear your head again, come to me."

"My dad told you," she said.

"He told me a great deal."

"You're not my father."

"Tessa, what I want to do to you is not fatherly. It's the furthest thing from fucking fatherly I can think of."

Her gaze went to his chest. "I ... I don't think I should work for you anymore."

"You're not leaving. That's not even going to be an option."

"Why are you being so difficult?"

"Why are you?"

"I'm not part of this world."

"Your father was."

"And he told me so much about it. You're going to have to marry within the family. to further your connections. This, it can't work. Please, don't make me become something I don't want."

He reached out, stroking his fingers across her flesh. She really was so beautiful, so soft.

She was everything he wanted in a woman, but within his world, he could get her killed.

A good man would send her away.

Would allow her to live a life that made her happy.

He wasn't a good man.

Nor a nice man.

He wanted her.

Plain and fucking simple.

There was no way he'd ever let her go, not without a fight.

Stroking his fingers through her hair, he tugged on the band that kept the long, brown locks in place.

It slid out with ease, and he cupped the back of her head, tilting it back so that he could stare into her eyes.

"I'll never make you become something you don't want, Tessa. I don't get to be told what to do."

"But you're going to get married."

"I'm still very much single. Unless you have something in mind. We could leave right now. Go to Vegas. You could be mine by the end of the day."

She shook her head.

He leaned in close.

"No one else tells me what to do. If I want to marry you, I'll marry you." He pressed a kiss to her cheek.

He heard her indrawn breath and smiled. She really was so sweet and caring.

Watching her with Caesar, it had been next to impossible for him to not claim her.

He wanted to fuck her.

To take her.

To make her his.

In his world, he didn't wait around for the right moment; he took. Moving to her lips, he stared into her eyes and then took her lips. Her hands left the chains and gripped his shoulders.

As he bit down on her lip, she let out a little cry, and her mouth opened. Unable to resist, he slid his tongue in, tracing across her teeth and meeting her.

She stroked him back, and he deepened the kiss, drawing her off the swing and into the warmth of his body. His cock stirred, and if they were back at home, he'd have taken that precious virginity of hers.

He wasn't a good man or a kind man, but Tessa made him do crazy-as-fuck things.

"Sir, you have reservations at the restaurant," Cole said.

Breaking from the kiss, he tucked Tessa's head against his chest. He didn't respond to Cole.

Tessa breathed deeply. One of her hands splayed across his chest.

"Reservations?"

"You've been out most of the day. I told Louise not to bother with making us food. Come on, let's go and eat."

She tugged on his hand. "I can't."

"Why not?"

"I'm not dressed."

He smiled. "You don't have to worry about a thing." He walked back to the car, still holding her hand. Opening the door, he helped her inside. Cole and Demetri both sat at the front.

He wouldn't allow there to be any distance between himself and Tessa. Wrapping an arm around her shoulders, he pulled her close.

"I miss my dad," she said, the moment the car started moving.

"I do as well."

"Did you like him?" she asked.

"I adored your father. He was a good man. A strong man."

"A bit of a joker as well," Cole said.

He'd not put up the partition.

"Your father was well-liked, Tessa," Demetri said. "We all lost a part of ourselves the day he was taken."

She nodded, but she didn't try to fight him.

They arrived at Louis's restaurant, which had been repaired from its latest vandalism attempt.

As always, the place was thriving. Louis served the best Italian cuisine around at affordable prices. It's one of the reasons Alonzo invested in the place when he first needed some startup capital to help. Cole and Demetri sat at the bar while he helped Tessa into his usual booth.

"I don't mind if you want them to sit with us."

"I want you all to myself."

"I think at times you're expecting something from me, and I don't know what it is. I know you've been nice to me since my father's passing, but how long is that going to last?"

"You think the only reason I want you is out of respect for your father?"

She shrugged. "Isn't it?"

He chuckled. "You've got a lot to learn about men."

"I have?" She tilted her head to the side.

"Yes. Men who just respect your father wouldn't buy you a whole new wardrobe for you to look nice in."

"I'm returning those clothes. I can't afford them."

"You return those clothes and I'll chain you to my bed and spank your ass."

"You'd beat me?"

"No, not a chance. I'd never put a bruise on that skin. First, I'd get you so hot for me. Your pussy would be dripping for me and only for me. I'd get you ready to take my dick. To fuck you. When I slapped your ass, giving you the spanking you deserve, you'd be ready for it, baby. You'd be ready for me to fuck you, to take you so hard that you were screaming for me to not stop."

Her eyes had dilated, and she pressed her thighs together. Her body begged for it.

"You say a lot of dirty things."

"And you love it, Tessa. You can deny it if you want, but your body, it wants to be fucked. It screams for my cock."

"So, all you want to do is fuck me?" she asked.

Her cheeks were so pretty being bright red.

"Look at you, saying naughty words. I want to drive my cock inside you, feel you come all over it. Those lips, I want them wrapped around me when I take you, fucking your throat. I can't wait to suck on those tits as you ride my dick. I'll teach you everything you need to know."

"We shouldn't—"

"Why not? Tell me, Tessa, you've not thought about it? You've not thought about me being inside you. About being fucked. About taking my cock." He saw the answer was she had. She'd thought about him a whole lot. He smiled. "Don't worry, I'll never take what you're not willing to give."

The waiter brought over their menus at his signal.

He knew how to work with her kind of need.

Chapter Six

The meal was perfect, as Tessa had no doubt it would be. Alonzo was known for his perfectionist side. He loved a good meal, and she'd listened to Louise talk about his appetite many times in the kitchen.

On the way home, there was a tension in the car. She didn't know what caused it. She kept glancing up at him, and his gaze would follow her everywhere.

Biting her lip, she tried not to smile, not to give in to the need to have him so close to her.

Everything he said at the restaurant had only served to turn her on more. She didn't know it was possible to feel this needy, this desperate, this hungry for him.

Pushing some hair out of her face, she tried to think of something else. Only, the hands that rested on his thighs kept drawing her attention in the reflection of the mirror.

They were large hands, and the way they felt on her body last night had been sheer perfection.

Cole and Demetri sat up front once again, and it kept her from speaking aloud. She wanted to ask him so many questions, and yet, she couldn't bring herself to say a single one.

Alonzo pulled her close, his lips against her ear.

"Do you think I can't see what you're thinking about? What you want? I see you staring at me, and you want me, don't you?"

She nodded her head.

"Are you ready for me to fuck you?"

Even as she was scared, she didn't want to wait anymore. "Yes, I'm ready."

"Good. Because I want you."

He took hold of her hand, locking their fingers

together. Her heart raced, and she didn't pull away.

The drive seemed to take forever.

When they finally pulled up to the driveway, Alonzo opened the door the minute the car stopped. He didn't let go of her hand, or stop to speak to anyone else. He kept hold of her hand, leading her into their home and straight up the stairs.

The soldiers saw her, and she passed Michele on the stairwell, hanging off another man. The glare she got chilled her to the core, but she ignored it.

Alonzo walked her to his quarters.

Jessica had pointed them out to her and warned her to never enter.

Within seconds she was inside. The door closed, and she pressed up against it.

"You're mine now, Tessa. Coming with me like this, telling me you want me, there's no backing out. Once I take you, you'll be mine. You'll be bound to me."

"I thought I already was." He'd taken her in, cared for her.

He pushed the jacket from her shoulders, followed by her shirt.

She reached out for him, attacking his buttons. Alonzo swatted her hand out of the way as she pulled it up over his head, exposing his body to her gaze.

Covered in ink, every single part of him was rock-hard. Unable to resist, she reached out, running her hands up his chest to circle his neck.

"You have no idea how much I've wanted to feel your hands on me."

In swift, easy moves, he had her completely naked, and he swung her up in his arms, carrying her through his main sitting room, going to his bedroom.

He dropped her down on the bed. He didn't move away just then. She kept her legs wrapped around his waist, not wanting to let go. Even though she wanted this, the nerves were back in full force.

Alonzo kissed her, but this time it wasn't a lingering kiss. He trailed down to her neck, sucking on her pulse before gliding down to her tits.

"You have no idea how much I've been wanting to suck on these tits. Last night was just a taste."

"Why did you leave me last night?" she asked.

"I'm not a good man, Tessa. There's only so much control I have. Your body, I've wanted you for a long time now. That day I saw you, you were only eighteen, and I wanted you. Even as you sobbed in my arms, losing control. I wanted you."

She cried out as he circled one of her nipples before moving to the next, his teeth biting into her flesh. She rocked her pussy against him, the fabric of his trousers rubbing against her clit.

It wasn't enough. She wanted his cock deep inside her, sliding in. Fucking her. For two years, Alonzo had wanted her.

He'd waited for her.

Not once in those two years had she seen him with another woman. Even when she thought he was going to make her leave, he'd given her the job as Caesar's nanny. He'd kept her close by, and it did things to her heart, knowing he cared enough about her to make her stay.

Sinking her fingers into his hair, he began to move down her body until he got to her pussy. He gripped her thighs, holding them open.

"You've got the prettiest pussy I've ever seen."

"I bet you say that to all the women."

"None of the women have ever had my mouth on them." His tongue slid between her folds, teasing her clit. "None of them will ever know pleasure from me."

"I don't want to talk about them," she said, feeling that spark of jealousy she promised to never have.

He held open the lips of her pussy as he began to suck on her clit, biting down on her flesh, going back and forth. The pleasure was so intense.

"Good, because they are not worth your time to even think about. They were just whores, Tessa. They meant nothing to me. You, you're everything."

He moved down to circle her entrance, but he didn't penetrate her. He teased her pussy. Each time she got close to her orgasm, he'd pull away, making her wait.

It drove her wild, wanting him.

She screamed his name, not caring how needy she sounded. All she could think about was his tongue on her clit.

He stroked back and forth over her nub, repeating the same action, making her ache for more, hungry for him, desperate.

"Please, please," she said.

"I know what you need, and when you come, I want you to scream my name. No one else, just me."

He sucked on her hard, and the pain and pleasure mingled together. She couldn't think. Everything was blurred, and then, he threw her over the edge.

His name spilled from her lips as she cried out for more, her body floating as wave upon wave of incredible pleasure consumed her. She'd never experienced anything like it before in her life. He didn't let up.

Even as she begged him to stop, he held her still and continued teasing her pussy. She didn't think it was possible to find another release.

Alonzo didn't give her a second one.

Panting for more, he moved between her thighs. During the time he gave her an orgasm and worked her up to the edge of a second, he'd removed his pants. His cock pressed against her slit, the bulbous head right there at her entrance.

She was so horny.

Hungry for his touch.

So desperate to feel that peak once again that as he slammed in deep, tearing through her virginity, the pain took her by surprise. She hadn't expected to feel the scorching heat as his cock filled her, shocking her. She cried out his name, only this time, there was no pleasure. Just sheer agony.

He held her down to the bed. His lips over hers, stealing every single cry, every pant.

Tears filled her eyes and spilled down her cheeks.

He'd taken her virginity.

Torn through her body.

Claimed her cherry, and no, there was no doubt who she belonged to.

He took her hands, pressing them to the bed, locking her in place.

"I know it hurts, but after this time, it won't hurt again, I promise."

Alonzo pulled out of her until only the tip remained. The pain had lessened some, and it took her breath away as he pushed inside her.

With every thrust of his cock, the pain seemed to disappear. It wasn't the best experience in the world, but it wasn't the worst either.

She'd been so wet, and he wasn't a small man. If he'd not gotten her ready for his cock, it would have really fucking hurt, no doubt about it.

The tears dried up on her face, and he reached between them, teasing her clit.

Tessa didn't think it was possible to find orgasm, but she should have known that Alonzo didn't give up without a fight.

He teased her clit, bringing her closer and closer to her release until she finally split apart, his cock driving inside her as he fucked her.

Once.

Twice.

Three times.

He erupted his seed deep, and she took every single drop.

****

Later that night, Alonzo stroked a hand down her stomach, running his fingers between her spread legs. He wouldn't have her hiding from him. After he'd taken her virginity, he'd treated her like a queen, carrying her to his bathroom, making sure she was cared for. She'd winced when he placed her in the water.

The first time for a woman was never easy. He'd never cared if a woman enjoyed their experience with him or not. They were there to satisfy him. Of course, most women he used in this life knew the score. They weren't special, would never be special. They were merely vessels to be used for a release, nothing more.

As his father once said, cum dumps.

That's what his father called them.

Shaking his head, he teased through her slit, touching her pussy. She released a little gasp, and he couldn't help but smile.

While she'd been in the bath, he'd cleaned the sheets from the bed. The blood had made him pause. Some women didn't bleed on their first time. Seeing the evidence of Tessa, it opened something primal within him.

"You've got to promise me that if anything happens to me, you'll protect her."

"Nothing's going to happen to you."

"I'm old, son. Getting older. I've kept Tessa from

the real world so long. She doesn't always know the danger that surrounds us. Without anyone to take care of her, she's going to get hurt. Promise me."

"I promise you, Tessa will be protected."

He'd intended to put her in an apartment. Pay for all of her needs and let her live her life. The day she'd come home from school and he had to tell her about her parents, it had broken a part of him.

She wasn't like anyone he'd ever met. Their life made them hard. Even Jessica held a bitterness, and for the most part, they'd tried to keep her safe and protected.

"I love that you're wet for me." He slid a finger in deep. "I want you to start wearing those skirts I spent a fortune on."

"I asked you not to spend so much."

"I like spending money on you." He added a second finger and began to finger-fuck her. In and out. She whimpered, arching up, crying out his name as he fucked her. She was so incredibly tight.

In and out.

In and out.

He pressed a thumb to her clit and began to stroke back and forth, watching her. Some of his cum still leaked out of her pussy. There was no way he'd wear a condom with her. When they were together, he wanted them to be as close as possible.

She started to rock on his fingers as he stroked her clit. When she was close, he pulled his fingers from her pussy and sat at the head of the bed.

"What are you doing?" she asked as he reached her.

He took her hand, placing it on his shoulder before he gripped her hips, guiding her over his lap, to straddle his waist. She followed his instructions, and he groaned as her pussy pressed against his cock. He was already so hard for her.

"You're going to be the one in control this time."

"I don't think I can."

He held his cock, lifting her up. "Use me to hold yourself up."

She did, and he placed his cock at her entrance. With the tip leaking pre-cum over the head, he got her to lower her body over his dick.

Inch by glorious fucking inch, she sank down until he was nearly at the hilt. With most of his cock inside her, he held both of her hips, guiding her down his length. At the last few inches, he took over, grinding his cock up as he drew her down.

They both groaned as her nails sank into the flesh of his shoulders.

"Fuck, that feels so good," he said.

Tessa rested her head on his shoulders. She took several deep breaths before sitting up. Her eyes were a little glazed over as she smiled at him.

"I want you to come here," he said.

"Here?"

"Every single night. You're mine. The moment you enter my quarters, strip."

"I can't do that."

"If you don't, I'll put you over my knee and give that pretty ass of yours a nice good spank." He gripped her ass, thrusting up inside her, hitting a spot deep that was both pain and pleasure. He smiled as she moved with him, her body taking over.

She rocked on his cock, moaning his name, the sound sweet music to him as she took her pleasure.

He wanted to hear her come, to relish every sound of her release. She was fucking beautiful and pure.

He'd make her love sex, to love taking his cock. When he finally gave her his name, she'd love him more than anything else in this world, and she'd be completely devoted to him and no one else.

Some men saved their devotion for their mistress. Their wives were meant for breeding. He intended for Tessa to be everything. The wife by his side, the whore in the bedroom, and the perfect mother to his kids.

A man who spread his life between women was weak. His mind wasn't in the game. Having everything in one package, it would keep them both safe.

"Touch yourself, Tessa. Show me how you stroke your pussy."

"I'm never having sex while I do it."

"Now you can feel how good it is to have both. Come on, baby. Show me."

Her hand moved from his shoulders, sliding down his chest. The action was so slow but so tempting. She drove him crazy, and there was no other way to describe it. When it came to Tessa, she fucking completed him.

When she cupped between her thighs, with how he had her straddling, the slit of her pussy was open. He watched her touch her clit.

At first, she only used one finger to tease herself. When that wasn't enough, a second finger moved between her wet slit, going back and forth.

She let out a gasp, crying out as she stroked herself. With each touch to her nub, her cunt tightened around his cock, squeezing his balls.

Closing his eyes, he gritted his teeth, counting to ten. Before he came, he wanted to feel her tight pussy on his cock.

He didn't get a chance to bask in the pleasure during the first ride of her pussy, but he wanted it now.

Her tits bounced with every thrust, and he took one of her rock-hard nipples between his teeth, biting down on the delicious mound. She tasted fucking sensational.

With her tight heat wrapped around his length, her hand on her pussy, and just the pleasure itself, he was so close to the edge.

The moment she came, it was sweet relief to him.

Her pussy pulsed around his cock, and it set off his own climax. Every time her pussy tightened it was like she milked his balls of his cum.

The last time he'd checked her medical records, she'd not been on any form of contraception. If he kept coming inside her, it would only be a matter of time before she got pregnant

He wanted her to have his kid, to take his seed, to swell with their child.

As she collapsed against him and he held her close, it was like an urge overcame him. It made him desperate for more.

Pulling her head back from his chest, he stared into her eyes, and then took possession of her lips. So perfect, so sweet, and he was hungry for more.

Sliding his tongue across her lips, he stayed within her.

"Is it always like this?" she asked.

"Like what?"

"So perfect?"

"You think I'm perfect."

"You're really something, you know that already though."

He winked at her. Kissing her lips, he let her get comfortable, with her head against his chest, her hands wrapping around him.

"I don't want to leave this moment."

"Then don't. We can stay like this for the rest of the night." He kissed her head. She'd be in his bed for the rest of her life.

Tessa may not know it yet, but she was falling for him. No doubt about it.

She got heavy on his chest, and as he stared down into her eyes, he saw she'd fallen asleep. His cock was already stirring to life for round three, but he didn't push. Instead, he held her close.

He'd never slept with a woman before in his life. Too many people wanted him killed.

So even as he'd claimed her virginity, Tessa was about to be his first, and she didn't even know it yet. He closed his eyes and fell asleep.

Chapter Seven

The following day, Tessa smiled at Caesar as he crawled across the carpet. They were in Jessica and Benedict's quarters. For once, Jessica actually sat on the floor with them. Her hair was pulled up off her face, and she was smiling at her son.

"I can't believe he's getting so big," Jessica said.

"It won't be long until he's walking, that's for sure." She tucked some hair behind her ears as Caesar stopped halfway. He sat back on his bottom and pressed his hands together, looking so cute. Seconds later, he started again, heading straight for Jessica.

The moment he was at Jessica's thighs, she smiled down at her son. "Well done. Off you go."

Caesar didn't like that, so he crawled into his mom's lap, taking a seat.

"I think someone doesn't like you saying no," Tessa said.

"Story of my life. Another man that doesn't like no."

Tessa saw the happiness die in Jessica's eyes, but she didn't push Caesar away. Instead, she placed a hand on her child's stomach and made sure he was safe.

"You know there was a time I was jealous of you."

"Of me?"

"Yes. I mean, I know your father was a soldier and all that, but you seemed to have everything. Your father adored you. Your mother was devoted to you. You could have any life you wanted."

"My parents died, Jessica."

"I know. You didn't have to stay here though."

"I didn't? I hate to break it to you, I didn't have a choice. Alonzo … I mean, Mr. Zanetti, told me it wasn't safe."

"My brother has had an obsession with you for some time now. It's kind of scary when I think about it."

"I don't think that's true."

Jessica chuckled. "I've seen the way he looks at you. We don't even need Michele here, but he keeps her around so he can have you."

Tessa stared down at Caesar. "Would you like me to leave?"

"You're the only person in this family that hasn't judged me for my decisions. For what I told you." Jessica looked at her.

The pain in her eyes struck Tessa hard.

"You have no idea what that means to me," Jessica said.

"I don't think you hate your son," Tess said. "I think … you don't want to get attached to him because they're going to take him away."

Tears filled Jessica's eyes, and before she caught them, some leaked out.

"I'm such a mess."

"He's your son," Tessa said.

"The moment he was born a boy, he stopped being my son."

"You can't let them do this."

"I don't have a choice. My mother warned me, and look at Alonzo. He was never allowed near me. There are times he is more a stranger to me than a brother."

Tessa was about to go and give her hug when the sound of a door being slammed open and Benedict's angry growl filled the air.

Jessica quickly handed Caesar back to her and got to her feet.

"Where are you, bitch?" The door opened, and

Benedict, looking so filled with rage, advanced toward Jessica. "You think you can just do what you like, is that it? You think your pussy is made of gold."

"Go, Tessa. Take Caesar to play."

She hesitated.

"Now!"

"Get the fuck out," Benedict said.

Being yelled at always made her cry, so as she made her way to the door, tears filled her eyes. Caesar started to whimper.

The sound of flesh hitting flesh cut Tessa to the core. She couldn't stop Jessica from getting hit, but she wasn't going to stand by and let anything happen to her. Running out of Jessica's quarters, she charged down the main stairs. Without waiting for an invitation, she pushed past three guards and walked straight into the library.

Alonzo sat with Demetri, Cole, and a couple of other men.

The moment he caught sight of her, he got to his feet.

"You're not supposed to be here."

"You have to stop him." Alonzo grabbed her arm and marched her out of the library. The door slammed closed with a resounding thud. "Stop. Listen to me, Alonzo."

"It's Mr. Zanetti right now, Tessa. Remember that."

"Stop it. You have to go to Jessica."

"What the fuck has my sister done now?" he asked.

"Benedict is hurting her."

Alonzo just stood there. "She's his wife, Tessa. There's nothing I can do."

She stared at him in shock. "You're not going to do anything?"

"There's nothing I can do. What goes on between a man and his wife, stays there."

"She's your sister."

"My hands are tied."

She couldn't believe what she was hearing. There's no way he could be saying these things, let alone believe them.

"I can't … that's not possible."

"Go and take care of Caesar. I'll see you tonight."

Benedict could be killing her. Raping her.

She had walked away.

"Dad, do you ever stop what you know to be wrong even if it'll get you in trouble?" she asked.

"That's a tough one. If you see something that you know to be wrong and you can stop it, and you feel you can't walk away, then you're not going to be able to live with yourself. You have to do what is right. Even if it's scary, you have to step up."

She pushed Caesar into Alonzo's waiting hands. Even as tears poured down her face, she was so angry and disgusted with him. She didn't care that they were in front of witnesses or that he was the boss.

"You're a coward."

She turned on her heel, and before he could stop her, she ran back up in the direction of Jessica's quarters.

Hearing the truth spill from Jessica's lips a few days ago, knowing she wanted to love her son but couldn't, it had changed something within her.

Maxwell Brown didn't raise his daughter to be a coward.

He raised her to do the right thing, to know right from wrong.

A man beating up a woman, that was fundamentally wrong. But for her, what made it even more so was Alonzo doing nothing.

She didn't know if he followed her or what would happen for her disrespect. All she knew was she had to make Benedict stop.

Stepping into Jessica's quarters, she heard the cry, the unmistakable sound of a punch hitting flesh.

Grabbing the lamp next to the door, she disconnected the cord and charged into the room. Jessica was curled up in a ball, and Benedict was on her, his knees keeping her locked into place as he drew his fist back and kept hitting her.

She'd had enough.

As he raised his fist, she used the lamp like a bat, slamming it against his face.

With a sickening thud, Benedict collapsed away from his wife. Panting for breath, Tessa stood over Jessica.

Jessica may be older than she was by nearly five years, but right there, Tessa would protect her as she would any child.

"Who the fuck do you think you are?" Benedict asked.

She may not have hit him hard enough.

"You're going to stop hitting her."

"She's my fucking wife. I'm an Adesso. You think you have power here? You're a fucking nanny. A piece of shit that is not even worth my time. They will have you spread for any man to fuck."

"I'm a Brown, and I will not stand by and watch you hurt her anymore."

He came toward her, clearly thinking she was joking, and she hit him again.

Just as he grabbed the lamp from her, Alonzo, Cole, and Demetri entered Jessica's quarters.

"It's about time you got here. Take this whore out of my rooms, now. I'm dealing with my wife."

"Get your hands off my woman, and leave my house."

Benedict let her go. He was in shock. Tessa stayed perfectly still, aware of Jessica between her thighs, in pain.

"You know the rules. No man interferes with his business with his wife."

"You had your hands on *my* woman, Adesso. To be honest, I think it's safe to say that this marriage between you and my sister is best put through the divorce courts."

"We don't divorce. Our families will never allow it."

"*I'm* the boss of my family, Benedict. You have brought me nothing but shame. Don't think I'm not aware of what you have at the docks. I am, and this, this is over. Get out."

"This isn't over," Benedict said.

"Oh, it is. I'll be talking with your father, so you better start kissing his ass."

When she felt it was safe, Tessa went to Jessica. The woman's face was bloody and bruised.

"It's okay. I'm here."

Ignoring Alonzo and the men, Tessa helped Jessica to her feet. She was holding her body.

"I'll call a doctor," Alonzo said.

She ignored him. He could call a doctor, but for now, she would take care of Jessica.

****

Alonzo finished the call with Benedict's father. By their mutual agreement, they would terminate the marriage and together they would form a united front to the rest of the families to make sure no disrespect was shown. Benedict's father wasn't aware of his son's extracurricular activities in working with the Russians on the trafficking market. Any business deals that required to go out of the family circle, had to be voted on. What Benedict had done was tell the families to fuck off in his ventures, and in doing so had provided Alonzo the ability to terminate his sister's marriage.

Now the only problem came with Caesar. Benedict had shown no love for the young boy, and after he saw Jessica's face and the doctor had informed him that she suffered from three broken ribs, there was no way he'd allow that bastard to have his nephew.

This was a fucking mess.

Leaving his office, he walked back to his sister's quarters. She was on the sofa, a bag of peas in her hand. The television was on, and he saw it was on a steamy romance.

"You still watch your trashy romance stuff," he said.

There was no sign of Tessa.

"If you're looking for Tessa, she's with Caesar in the nursery." She winced as she moved. She hugged a pillow against her.

"She hates me right now," Alonzo said, lowering himself into the chair opposite her.

Jessica kept wiping away her tears. "She doesn't understand our rules, Alonzo. You forget she's a soldier's daughter with his views and opinions."

"I should have stopped him."

"Alonzo," she said. "You and I both know no one could stop him. What is going to happen to Tessa? She's a sweet woman. Her heart is always in the right place. I hope you don't have to punish her too severely for helping me."

"She's not going to get punished, Jess."

"She's not?"

"No, and this marriage of yours, it's going to

end."

Jessica laughed. "Yeah, probably with me in a casket."

"No. I failed you today, and I've failed you a lot over the years. I know you didn't want this marriage. Dad was dying. I should have taken over sooner. It was his dying wish to bring us closer together. Benedict, he is an asshole."

"We can't have a divorce, you know that, Alonzo."

"I found out that Benedict was making deals with the Russians. He wanted in on their human trafficking. To bring men, women, and children, here, to use them. To sell them."

"Oh."

"It was a deal that wasn't accepted by any of us. None of the families would agree going into business with the Russians."

"They wouldn't?"

"No. We won't even work with the cartels, Jess. We're not going to work with Russians like that. It's not going to happen, so he's out. His father is pissed off."

"What about Caesar? He's a boy."

"He's your son, Jess. I wouldn't take him away from you. If you want him to live with Benedict, that is up to you."

"Are you going to marry me off anytime soon?" she asked. "Is this another part of a family expansion? Adesso wasn't good enough."

"You've got no reason to trust me."

"She came back, Alonzo. With a damn lamp, she came back for me. You didn't."

He'd had to make sure Caesar was safe before he followed Tessa. He was pissed that she'd gotten here before he had. How she stood over Jessica, she looked like a damn queen. He'd never seen her look so fierce. She was a force to be reckoned with.

"There are no excuses for my behavior. I'm only grateful that she got here in time before he did any real damage." He cupped his sister's face, careful not to be too hard to hurt her bruises. Seeing the damage that bastard had done to her pissed him off even more. Benedict wasn't finished receiving his punishment. The rules be damned. No woman deserved this kind of treatment and certainly not his sister, under his own roof.

"You care about her, don't you?" Jessica asked.

"I do. She means a great deal to me."

"She's not suited to this way of life, Alonzo. If you have any care at all, you'd let her go."

"Not going to happen."

"You're going to make her stay here?"

"I'm the only one that can make her happy."

"And what if the price of that happiness is her pain? Would you do that to her?"

He gritted his teeth, hating that his sister spoke … logically. "I'm not a good man. I know what I want."

"And to hell with everything else?"

"Be careful, Jessica."

"Do you even love her, or is it about claiming her innocence? Don't think I don't know what game you're playing. Benedict told me to men it's about the chase. About owning something you never had before."

"Don't listen to that asshole. He doesn't have the first clue what is going on here."

"And you do?"

"I know more than you think."

She scoffed. "Yeah, right."

"I'm not going to sit here arguing with you. Jessica, I love you. Words are not going to make up for the fact I wasn't here to protect you. I'll do everything I can from this day forward to keep you safe. That is my vow to you." He leaned forward and kissed her head, being gentle as always.

Getting to his feet, he left her quarters. He didn't want to hear what that piece of shit, Benedict had to say.

He didn't answer to anyone.

Not his father, who was very much dead.

His mother had run off when she couldn't take over everyone's life. She really had thought for a short time that she'd lead the Zanetti family. No woman had ever led this family, and no woman ever would.

It wasn't just about being sexist. A woman would be killed in less than a day. Their world didn't handle women leaders well. He'd seen some die in his time, and it was never pretty.

He made his way to the nursery where Tessa still was.

Again, no sign of Michele. That bitch didn't do anything unless it was to benefit her, and he was growing tired of all of her fucking games. He'd have her fired.

He stood outside the nursery. The guard was there, but all of them knew not to look at Tessa. Not to do anything for her unless she asked for it, and certainly not to get any ideas in thinking they had a chance with her.

Caesar was in his bed fast asleep while Tessa was curled up in her chair. It looked like she was crying. Entering the room, she turned to look at him with a gasp.

"I'm not here to argue with you or cause you any pain," he said.

"You'll wake him up."

"Then come with me."

She shook her head.

"Then I guess I'll wake him up. Either way, you're not escaping me."

"Why do you have to be so difficult? I can't just leave him."

He rolled his eyes and stepped out of the room, seeing the guard on duty. "Keep an eye on this little guy. If he wakes up, find his other nanny before I fire her ass. She gives you any problem at all, tell her I'm going to fire her." Which he would be doing regardless.

With that, he grabbed Tessa's hand, and didn't wait as he pulled her out of the room. When she started to struggle, he did no more than put her over his shoulder and carry her down the long corridor, heading toward his own space.

"Put me down." She slapped his ass, to which he did the same to hers. "Hey. That's not fair."

He slapped her ass again for good measure, and she let out a growl, which he found to be so cute.

Instead of slapping her ass again when she hit him, he started to caress each cheek.

"They are not yours to touch," she said.

He smirked. "Of course they are. They are no one else's, and last time I checked, I owned every single delicious curve on your body."

"Put me down, Alonzo. Take me to my room. I want nothing to do with you."

"No can do, I'm afraid. You're stuck with me."

"Why? I don't want this. I don't want to be with a man who can just stand by and let his sister get beaten."

That made his jaw clench because he didn't have a decent enough fight to defend himself. He hadn't known it was that bad. Men were not supposed to interfere with marriages like that. If it wasn't for Benedict's current fuck-up with traffickers, he would be the one in trouble.

Marriage was private.

In their world a man could do what he wanted

with a woman, consequences be damned. It wasn't like they could go to the cops about it. No one was to know.

Once he got to his quarters, he put her down on the floor and stepped back, watching her.

She had no idea the kind of monsters he dealt with.

Where his world was flooded in darkness, hers was all light. He couldn't let her go even though he knew it would make her happy. She'd find someone who was like her. Who loved. Who cared.

Letting her go wasn't an option for him.

Chapter Eight

Alonzo kept staring at her. Tessa didn't like being in his part of the house, nor did she like the way her body came alive under his touch, even after everything she knew about him. This wasn't what she wanted.

Part of her still wanted to hate him.

To be disgusted by what he allowed to happen under his roof.

Just one look at Jessica, a real look, he'd have seen the damage that bastard was doing. But … she had ignored it herself, and it sickened her.

Her father wouldn't have stood by.

"I'd like to leave," she said.

Alonzo shook his head. "That's not happening."

"Why?"

"You don't get to leave. You don't get to do that."

"I don't have some fancy name. I'm not part of this. I can leave if I want." She stared at him, and he put his hands in his pockets. He looked so damn attractive, so … Alonzo. Her body tightened. Her nipples puckered, and she felt an ache in her pussy.

This man had gotten under her skin.

He made her ache, made her want him even though every single part of her brain was screaming at her to get the hell out.

"I don't want to be part of this. You weren't going to do anything. You think I can stand around watching something like that?"

"We have rules we must follow."

"Screw the rules. You're saying if a wife was getting beaten and raped by her husband and you knew it, you'd not do anything? You'd not make it stop?"

"Tessa, you don't know the way our world

works."

"You wouldn't do anything!" She screamed each word.

"It can get us killed!" This time he yelled right back at her.

Tears filled her eyes, but she wasn't backing down. "No. I don't believe that. No man should be allowed to ever hurt a woman or to lay a hand on her."

"You think your father was any different?" he asked, advancing toward her.

She gasped. "Don't you dare bring him into this. He wouldn't have stood by."

"He did." Alonzo stood right in front of her.

"I don't believe you."

"Like all good soldiers and all good men that serve us, when it comes to a man and a woman, no one steps in. No one threatens war. Not over a woman. Do you even realize how many people will die if that happens?"

"I don't believe you."

"This world is full of bad men, Tessa. Bad men that do bad things. We're not good. I never claimed to be good, but I am not a coward. I will never back down from a fight or from a loved one. Your father, he was a good man, but he knew how the world works. You don't interfere, ever."

They were both panting, and she glared at him.

He held her arms, and she didn't even fight him. His eyes were so dark they were almost black.

Alonzo tugged her to him, and she cried out as his lips landed on hers. He gripped the back of her head, his fingers digging into her. She pushed against his shirt even as she moaned into his mouth.

The fight left her as his tongue traced across her lips, and she was kissing him back with a passion that startled her. She didn't want to let him go.

Alonzo walked them back until she was pressed against the hard wall, his body trapping her.

Within seconds he was tearing at her shirt, breaking the kiss so that he could lift it up over her head, tossing it to one side. His hands were on her waist, holding her in place as he attacked her mouth. It felt so good to be owned by him. To have him touching her, driving her wild, filling her with ecstasy.

She tugged on his shirt, buttons spraying everywhere.

With her nails, she scored his flesh, relishing his moans.

"Fuck, baby, that's it. I don't give a fuck if you hate me right now. Know that I'm not letting you go."

"I hate this world."

"Be my guest. You think I don't hate it? You think I like the rules?"

"Leave it then. Change it."

"I can't. The only way to leave the Zanetti is in death."

She didn't want him to die. Cupping his cheeks, she pulled him back in for a kiss. She couldn't think of him as being dead.

At this moment, she didn't like him, but she wouldn't wish him dead.

As she slid her tongue across his lips, he opened up, and she plunged inside, kissing him back.

Once again, Alonzo broke the kiss. He knelt down before her, cupping her ass as he tugged on the pants she wore. Kicking them to one side, he held one of her legs over his shoulder.

Her pussy opened, and as his mouth latched onto her clit, she cried out his name.

"Watch me lick this sweet pussy, Tessa. Watch

me own it." He slid his tongue between her folds, stroking over her clit then down to fuck inside her.

She wanted to close her eyes but also watch him.

His instructions were simple. She had to watch him touch her, to bring her body alight with his touch.

Fingers teased at her entrance, sliding in and out. She felt one digit, then a second before he had her stretched with three fingers. His lips were over her clit, sucking on it. The pleasure was intense, and she felt full but wanted his cock for depth. To feel him fucking her, taking her, driving her crazy with need.

"I could lick your cunt all day long, baby. So fucking good. So mine," he said, speaking against her pussy.

He pulled his fingers from her cunt and trailed them back, stroking over her anus. At first, she tensed, not really sure what the hell was going on. He didn't let up in touching her back there, even as he trailed his tongue to her entrance and fucked her with it.

In and out.

She cried out, gasping his name.

One finger stroking her ass pressed forward, and she cried out as he began to enter her. At first, it burned. She'd never had anyone tease her ass or stroke it.

The sensation was out of this world. She couldn't focus on anyone or anything. The wall wasn't enough support, and she clenched her hand into a fist.

"You like my finger in your ass, Tessa?" She couldn't answer him. "That's okay. Your body doesn't lie, and I know how much it's loving it. Your pussy is so wet. I can't wait to put my cock inside you."

She shook her head. "That's not possible."

He chuckled. "Oh, my sweet, little ex-virgin. You have no idea how very much possible it is. You pussy. Your ass. Your mouth. Even your tits can take my cock, and of course you can make me come with your hands. There's so much for you to learn, but you don't have to worry about a thing. I'm going to teach you everything."

His finger was all the way inside her ass, and he started to add a second. His tongue stroked over her clit.

There was pain, but it wasn't a bad kind of pain.

She loved the feeling of being full, but she wanted his cock inside her.

"My needy woman wants me, don't you?"

She bit her lip. How could he know exactly what she was thinking? Feeling? He couldn't be a mind reader.

He chuckled against her pussy, his tongue playing with her clit.

"I'm no mind reader, baby, but what I am, is right. You want me. You want my cock deep inside you." He pulled his fingers from her pussy and ass. "Take off my clothes."

With shaking fingers, she removed the rest of his clothes. The shirt was destroyed unless she sewed all the buttons back on it.

She could do it; she just didn't know if it would be something he would want.

"That's it. Now, my boxers."

He wore a pair of black boxer briefs. The hard ridge of his cock was outlined in the front. He was so long, so thick, and she wanted to taste him the way he had her. When she pulled the boxers from his body, his cock stood out. The tip was already slick with pre-cum, and it seemed to pulse.

Staring at it now, she had to wonder how he fit inside her.

"You want to taste my cock, baby?"

She stared up at him. Kneeling on the floor in front of him, she wondered just how much of this man she could truly possess.

****

Every single time she nibbled her lip, it made Alonzo's cock ache to be inside her mouth. Wrapping his fingers around his dick, he watched her.

Tessa couldn't help but watch him as he played with himself.

"Open your lips."

He expected her to deny him, to give him a bit of a fight. Like always, Tessa surprised him.

She opened her lips, and he stepped forward, placing his cock at her mouth.

Suddenly, she pulled away. "I don't know what I'm doing."

Now that as a prelude to a blowjob was one of the sexiest things he'd ever heard. "I'll tell you what to do."

He loved how fucking innocent she was. She belonged to him, and right now, she could hate him. It wasn't like he was happy with everything that went on in his world.

"Open your lips," he said.

She did the same as before. Her eyes were on him as he placed the head at her mouth.

"Don't use your teeth. Just feel it." He slid in a couple of inches.

Her eyes seemed to go wide. He pulled out.

"You're so big."

"That's what every man wants to hear." He saw her pretty little blush. "I won't hurt you. Remember that."

With his cock back in her mouth, he rocked back and forth, allowing her to get accustomed to the feel of him.

"Give me your hand."

He placed her hand around his length.

"Touch me, Tessa. I want to feel you enjoying

this as much as I am. Your hands and mouth feel so fucking good."

Her tongue licked over his hole, and she moaned around his length.

Gritting his teeth, he focused on instructing her, on telling her what he wanted and how he wanted it rather than just filling her mouth full with his cum.

She was so new at this.

It shouldn't feel this good.

It's because she is so different.

She's not like other women.

You like her, asshole.

Stroking her hair back from her face, he thrust a bit more until he hit her throat. Again, another moan, and as he his cock got deep again, she swallowed.

Wrapping her hair around his fist, he didn't tighten his hold, but he guided her over his cock, taking more of him.

Without his instruction, she began to move her hand up and down over his dick, working his cock.

Pumping into her mouth, he knew it wasn't going to be long before he came. He'd rather have his cum in her pussy where he could get her pregnant, but stopping right now was not possible.

His balls tightened.

"Baby, I'm going to come in your mouth. Don't swallow. Just don't fucking swallow."

He saw stars as he came.

Holding his cock against her lips, he spilled his release into her mouth, wave upon wave flooding her. He saw his cum filling her. She didn't swallow one drop.

Once he was done, he pulled back.

"Show me."

She tilted her head back and let him see.

"Now swallow."

She closed her mouth, and he watched her throat working.

"Show me."

She opened her lips, and there was her empty mouth.

"Good girl. My turn." He picked her up, helping her to her feet, walking her back until they were in his bedroom.

Dropping her on the bed, he followed her down, taking one of her hard nipples into his mouth. He sucked on it, flicking his tongue across the peak before biting down onto it.

She cried out, her back arching up.

Sliding a hand down her body, he cupped her between her thighs, finding her wet heat. She coated his fingers with her cream, and he groaned. "I love how wet you are for me." He sucked on her other nipple, working two fingers inside her greedy pussy.

She rocked back and forth, her fingers running through his hair, gripping tightly to the strands.

He didn't linger too long at her tits, kissing down her body, past her belly button and between her thighs.

Spreading the lips of her sex open, he teased her clit, circling the hard bud. She tasted so damn good.

He was already addicted, and would be doing this again and often.

Gliding his tongue down, he plunged inside her.

His cock was already hard again. He wanted to take her. To fuck away all of their problems. To forget what had happened today.

Pressing a kiss to her clit, he flipped her over with his hands on her hips.

"What are you doing?" she asked.

He didn't answer her. Gripping his cock, he placed it at her entrance and slid in. Her cries filled the air and he closed his eyes, basking in the pulse of her sweet cunt.

Caressing the curves of her ass, he opened his eyes as he spread her cheeks wide. His cock was nestled balls deep inside her pretty cunt.

When he slid out, her cream covered his length.

It was all the evidence he needed to know she wanted this. Regardless of what she was saying, she craved this.

Pulling out of her until only the head of his cock remained, he held her hips tightly as he fucked her, plunging in and out, not giving her a chance to get accustomed to his dick. Over and over he pounded her sweet pussy.

She grew wetter with each hard fuck inside her.

Stroking his fingers through her wetness, he drew them back to her anus, coating her once again.

He began to play with her asshole as he drove inside her. He pushed a single finger deep in her ass, working it in and out with the rhythm of his cock. She tightened around him.

"You see, Tessa, a virgin you may be, but I know what you crave. I know that even as you hate me or at least hate what I am, I know you want my cock. You want my lips. You want what only I can give you." Ramming inside her pussy, he relished her cries of passion. Each sound echoed off the walls, calling to him.

He was driven by her, wanting to fuck her, to drive her wild the way she did him.

"There's not going to be any other man for you, Tessa. I'm your fucking world now. If you think you can run from me, I'll find you. If you think there's someone else that could ever want you more, they can't. I fucking own you, every single part of you." He added a second finger to her ass. "And if I ever find another man who thinks he can lay his hands on you, I'll fucking kill him. Don't ever forget who you belong to, Tessa. You're mine. You'll always be mine."

With his other hand, he worked it between her thighs, stroking her clit.

She came with just a few strokes of his fingers, the sounds of her pleasure driving his own. He fucked her with his fingers in her ass. One day, he'd fuck her ass. He'd work his dick inside every single part of her.

Closing his eyes, he slammed in once more, and spilled his seed deep inside her pussy. He held himself to the hilt, hoping that this time she fell pregnant. It would be so much easier to keep her if she did.

He waited for her to take every single drop of his cum before pulling away.

As he did so, some of his seed fell out, and he pushed it back inside her, needing to mark her as his own.

"I'll be back."

He left her on the bed, going to the bathroom. Washing his hands, he dampened a towel and took it out to the bedroom.

Tessa was tiptoeing out of the room.

"Seriously?" he asked.

She didn't get far as she tried to run. He wrapped an arm around her waist, picked her up, and carried her to the bed.

He pushed her on her stomach. Keeping one hand near her neck, he used his other to lift her. Wiping her pussy of his excess cream, he then worked on her ass, cleaning her up from her own cum. With that out of the way, he tossed the towel away, wrapped his arms around her, and held her close.

"You can hate me, Tessa. I expect you to. I told you, I'm not a good man, but you're not going."

"You can't keep me here against my will."

He chuckled. "You seem to like telling me what I can and cannot do. You should learn by now that I do what I want."

"You're impossible."

"Admit it, Tessa. You want me."

She stayed silent.

"Okay, admit you don't like me."

She didn't say anything.

He laughed. "You're so damn stubborn." He kissed her neck. "Don't worry. I can work with stubborn."

"Why can't you let me go?" she asked.

"Because deep down, I know you don't want that." And neither did he.

Chapter Nine

Three days later

"I think it's cute," Jessica said.

Tessa glanced over at the other woman as Caesar wriggled between them. She'd brought him out into the gardens that afternoon. After ten minutes of him on the grass, Jessica had joined them.

Michele as usual was nowhere to be found. She hadn't seen her in a couple of days, but other than the nights when Alonzo fucked her brains out in his bedroom, she'd not seen him.

"What's cute?"

"Alonzo. I saw the flowers on the table, read the card. It's so sweet that he's trying to win you over, you know. It is a little funny that he'd try and do it. Most of the time women always fell all over themselves trying to impress him. Not you. You're outside, taking care of my son."

"Would you like me to leave?" Tessa said. "I know this job wasn't supposed to be long-term."

"You're not going anywhere, and I can't help you out. I'm guessing Alonzo considers you a flight risk. All of the guards have probably been threatened with their own death if they allow you to escape."

"I don't want to be a prisoner."

"From what I saw this morning of my brother pinning you against the wall, you weren't exactly fighting. For a prisoner, you looked really damn cozy."

"I'm shiny and new. He just wants to play with me until he grows bored." She averted her gaze.

What was happening between her and Alonzo, she didn't know. He was everywhere. Even when he wasn't close by, he seemed to sense her need for him. He'd call her or someone would stop by with a gift for her.

The roses he sent today, they were so sweet.

Dear my sweet,

I'm always thinking of you. Until tonight.

Love, Alonzo

The card had been so sweet, so simple, and yet, it spoke volumes to her.

"My brother does not care about shiny new toys, Tessa. Believe me, he's not besotted with you because of that. You frown a lot for someone so young."

"I don't know what any of this means at all. I've never dated, let alone had a boyfriend." She picked up one of Caesar's toys. The young boy saw it and came crawling toward her. She smiled as he reached out for it, and she let him take it. "What do you mean about him being besotted?"

Jessica chuckled. "You caught that bit, right?"

Her cheeks heated.

"You know, I really like you, and I can see why my brother likes you. I know I was going to have to marry someone I didn't want. In our world, we don't marry for love." Jessica shrugged. "You're different. You don't judge anyone. You take care of Caesar, and you're nice to everyone. I've seen the way Michele is. If they're not high enough on the food chain, she treats them like shit."

"I don't like being mean," Tessa said.

"It's not about being mean. You're a breath of fresh air in a world full of hate and betrayal."

Tessa stared down at the ground. "But it's not going anywhere."

"Why not?"

"You said yourself. This world doesn't allow love matches, and I don't want to be the other woman. I don't bring anything to this relationship. I don't give him money or power. I'm no one."

"You're far from being no one, Tessa. You're here, and he's not been with another woman."

"You don't understand," Tessa said.

"I do understand."

"How can I let him pick me when I know there is someone else who can give him what he needs?"

Jessica picked up Caesar and held him against her chest. "Alonzo won't marry out of duty, Tessa."

"You did."

"I'm a woman. Our father is dead. All the decisions land on Alonzo. He's the one in charge."

"I just don't see marriage being there for us."

"Why not?"

She didn't have an answer. Wasn't it too fast to assume marriage? She wasn't part of his world, not really.

"I think my brother is falling for you, Tessa."

"It's too soon."

"Just because he's been pursuing you for a couple of weeks doesn't mean he wasn't thinking about it long before then."

"What do you mean?"

"I know my brother. He's had his eye on you for some time." Jessica winked at her. "You were grieving your parents' loss. Going through so much pain and of course he was dealing with his own stuff. The time was not right, but now it is. Think about it, Tessa."

Tilting her head to the side, she stared at Jessica.

It seemed surreal to her that she was talking about this with anyone, let alone Jessica.

"Now, I think it's time that I took you for a nap. Don't you, sweet boy?"

"I can do that," Tessa said.

"Nope. I can, and my brother is heading this

way." Jessica got to her feet. "Besides, I think I'd like to try being a mom, even just once."

Before she could offer again, Alonzo was there, by her side. Tessa had already stood.

Cole and Demetri kept their distance, but like always, they were close.

"Did I miss something?" Alonzo asked.

"Not much. You look like you've had a shitty day. I'm taking Caesar in for his nap."

"I don't mind doing it," Tessa said.

"Please, you do enough around here, and I've taken up too much of your time already. Take care of her, Alonzo," Jessica said.

Tessa watched as Jessica carried Caesar into the house.

She didn't know what to say to him. Glancing over his shoulder before looking at her feet, she wondered what to do.

"I've missed you," Alonzo said.

She returned his gaze. "I liked the flowers."

"You did?"

"Yes, they were beautiful."

"Good. I picked them out especially for you."

"You did?" she asked.

"Don't sound so surprised. I can do a few things for myself. So, I was thinking we could go out dancing tonight."

"Dancing?"

"At a nightclub. I've already bought you a dress."

"Do you think it's safe?" She didn't want him to get hurt.

"With me around, it's always safe."

"Do you really want to take me with you? To be seen with me?" she asked.

This made him stop. "Why do I feel there's

something more going on right now?"

"I'm your ... help. I work for you. I'm not stunning or beautiful. Shouldn't you be seen out with women that stand out?" She hated speaking her doubts and her insecurities. It left a bad taste in her mouth.

Alonzo sighed. He cupped her face, and he was so close she felt his breath fan across her face.

"As far as I'm concerned, Tessa Brown, you are the most beautiful woman in the world. I want to be seen with you because you are mine. I want the world to know who you belong to. I'm not ashamed of who I want. I don't care what people think about you working for me or any of that bullshit. All I care about is you. Now, go upstairs and get ready. We leave in a couple of hours."

She chuckled, touched by his sweet words. "I don't need a couple of hours to get ready."

"You don't? How long do you need?"

"Ten, twenty minutes maybe."

His thumb stroked across her lip, and it was like he reminded her of how good his cock tasted filling her mouth. She touched his thumb with her tongue.

"Do you have anything in mind for how we could spend the next couple of hours?"

"You told me that you'd love to have me in the shower. Maybe you could show me how?" she asked.

"Look at you, my little temptress. Are you trying to seduce me?" he asked.

"That depends, is it working?" She didn't know where this need was coming from. He touched her, and her body went up in flames. The only man she wanted was him.

Feeling bold, she took his hand and led him past his guards. She didn't let him go as they walked through the house, past Louise the cook, and up to his quarters.

She didn't stop until she was in his bathroom.

Letting go of his hand, she pulled her dress up and over her head, letting it fall to the floor. She wore a pair of white panties and a sports bra. Stepping up close to him, she began to work his buttons open, taking her time, watching him through hooded eyes as he let her remove his clothes. The tension rose with every passing second.

Once he was completely naked, she removed her bra and panties. Presenting him her back, she reached out and put the shower on. Without waiting for him, she stepped beneath the warm spray. Tilting her head back, she felt him as he stood behind her. His hands wrapped around her, one moving between her thighs as the other cupped her neck. He held her tight against his body as he kissed her neck. The grip on her was intoxicating as he nibbled on her pulse.

"Baby, I can't be gentle right now."

"I don't need you to be gentle."

He tilted her hips, and his cock pressed between her thighs. He angled her hips so that he could thrust inside her.

She had no choice but to grip the shower wall as he fucked her.

He wasn't wrong about not being gentle.

Alonzo held her, his grip on the verge of pain. With every thrust inside her, his hold would tighten around her neck. She had no doubt he wouldn't hurt her.

He'd promised her he never would, and she believed him.

Putting her life in his hands was a heady experience.

She was at his mercy.

He controlled her.

Fucked her.

Ravaged her body.

His hand continued to tease her pussy as he drove inside her. His lips on her neck heightened her need until she came, screaming his name as her orgasm rushed through her body.

Alonzo wasn't far behind her, his grip never once loosening from her as he filled her body with more of his cum.

****

When he'd decided to take her out dancing, Alonzo had thought it would be a good idea, to see her outside of the house without the stresses that seemed to often plague her. However, he didn't sign up for her attracting any other attention. The dress he'd purchased for her was a deep blue one that molded to every single curve. Her ass looked so fucking hot and round. It called to have his hands all over it. Not to mention how her tits looked, squeezed together, showing a beautiful expanse of cleavage.

Jessica had come to the room to curl her hair. The brown locks were now glossy and curled.

She didn't wear any makeup as she simply didn't need it. There was no doubt about it. She was fucking stunning.

He'd ordered her an orange soda, as she didn't drink, and a whiskey for himself.

They were sitting in his VIP section, and they were getting looks from many people. Some of them he knew as sons from important families. Their daughters were not allowed here. Jessica, for instance, had never stepped foot in this place. Most wives were not allowed here either.

Speculation would be rife tomorrow.

His mistress?

His woman?

His whore?

Or just a plaything?

Tessa was everything.

She would be his queen one day.

He, Cole, and Demetri had already gone to pick out the ring. First, he wanted her to admit she'd fallen for him. He saw it in her eyes. The way she smiled at him. The touches, even Jessica had told him to be careful. Their little nanny had a delicate heart.

He knew.

"What do you think?" he asked.

"It's amazing. So much energy." She smiled at him. "I think this is my first time coming to a nightclub. Right now, I feel … buzzed." He took her soda from her, taking a sip. "What are you doing?"

"Checking to make sure I didn't give you the wrong drink."

She tapped his chest, laughing. "I'm not drunk."

He pulled her against his chest, cupping her cheek. "No, you're happy, and I like it."

Tilting her head back, he didn't care that others saw him with her. She was his woman, and he wasn't ashamed of her. He couldn't resist a kiss, and so right there, in front of everyone, he kissed her.

She didn't fight him. Her hand went to his shirt, the other tucked against his chest. She gripped him tightly. The little moan she released, he swallowed down.

So fucking tempting.

All his.

Forever and always.

He kissed down to her neck. "Do you have any idea how much I want to bend you over this table and fuck you?"

She gasped.

"Do you want that too?"

"Only if it was just us."

"Don't worry. As much as I want to fuck you, I won't. I'll contain my need for you, but be warned, baby, it's not fucking easy. Not even close." He growled against her neck, sucking on her pulse. "Come on, let's go and dance."

He took her hand, and leaving the VIP section, he took her to the dance floor. Drawing her ass against his dick, he wrapped his arms around her. Swaying from side to side, he placed a hand on his stomach and tilted her head back against him to stare into her eyes.

The rest of the world faded, and all that remained was the two of them. She consumed his entire world. Whenever he was with her, everything else just fell away. Nothing mattered. She filled his soul with everything he never thought it was possible to have.

"You're my world, Tessa Brown."

He didn't know when it had happened, but as clear as the day he was blooded into the mafia at his father's hand, he was in love with this woman.

No one else would ever be good enough.

Not a daughter of another family.

There's no way he'd ever shame this woman.

"Alonzo," she said.

"Yes, baby."

"I think I could get used to this, and it scares me."

"Why?"

"Jessica told me that your world doesn't do love." She stopped, and he saw her swallow. Saw the tears in her eyes. "And I'm afraid that I've already fallen for you."

"Fallen in love?"

She nodded.

His heart pounded. He'd been waiting so long for her, and it was like he'd already lived two lifetimes already.

"Don't be afraid."

"You can't love me back."

"Not only do I love you back, but I'm not going anywhere else."

"But, don't you have to marry someone important? Someone who will help your family, not hinder it."

He spun her around so that she now faced him. "There's no one around to tell me what to do. You're going to be my wife, Tessa. I love you more than anything else, and your father, he asked me if anything ever happened to him, I'd take care of you. I'm going to do that. Not because he asked me but because I can't let you go. Do you think I've not tried to let you go? Believe me, I have. Bringing you home with me, I wasn't supposed to keep you. I was going to let you go, but I loved seeing you around the house. Even miserable, I knew I had to keep you safe. All my other plans, they went out the window."

"I can't believe we're discussing this on the dance floor," she said.

He saw her sniffle, and he wiped the tears from her eyes.

The song changed, and he made her dance with him. He wasn't going to bring this night to a close just because he wanted to take her to bed. There would be time for that soon.

This wasn't how he was going to propose.

"Are you going to give me my answer?" he asked.

"To what?" She frowned.

He pulled her in close once again, holding her back. His lips against her hair. "To marrying me."

"You proposed?"

"When I said you were going to be my wife, I

figured I already had?"

She gasped. "I ... I ... yes, I think so, yes."

He threw his head back and laughed. "You think so?"

"I've never been asked to be married before. What if you're wrong? What if I'm just new to you and you regret wanting to marry me?"

He sighed. Letting her go, he bent down on one knee.

People on the floor stepped away, giving him room.

The music came to a stop.

All eyes were focused on them.

Tessa stared around the room.

She looked like a deer caught in the headlights.

"Tessa Brown, the hardest woman in the world to date, will you please do me the honor of becoming my wife?" he asked.

They had an audience. If she denied him now, it would be the biggest humiliation to him.

Her lips moved, but he didn't hear what her reply was.

"I didn't catch that."

"Yes. I'll marry you. Yes. Yes."

He kissed her finger. "I've got the ring at home." He got to his feet, cupping her face once again. As his lips touched hers, the enter crowd went wild, cheering for the two of them.

"You did that on purpose," she said.

"Damn right. You're unpredictable, Tessa. I needed to know you'd say yes."

"What if your family doesn't like me? I'm the nanny."

"Look at my face. I really don't give a fuck what they think. They have my loyalty, my devotion, and I have proven myself time and time again. I really couldn't give a shit if they wanted me out. I'd have you. Besides, Jessica already adores you."

"What about … the Adesso family?" she asked.

"I don't think you have a fan in any of them."

She chuckled. "I don't want to cause you any trouble."

"How about I worry about the Adesso and the family stuff? You worry about me and we'll compromise."

"Okay, deal."

Chapter Ten

Four days later

Alonzo linked his fingers with Tessa's as they looked through the wedding magazine together. She'd been insistent on just going to court and signing their names on the dotted lines. He wouldn't have that.

"These are really expensive," she said.

"Money's not an object. You're going to wear a white gown, have bridesmaids. I know Jessica is really looking forward to it."

"I thought we agreed to a small event."

"We agreed whatever we like."

She rested her head against his chest. "And what I like?"

"Is silly. I'm not marrying you like that where we exchange rings, sign the paper, and be done with it." He cupped her cheek, and she lifted her head, looking at him. "What would your father have wanted?"

"That's not fair," she said with a groan, covering her face.

"Is that because he'd have wanted his little girl to have a huge day where she was the star?"

"Yes."

"See, I know what you want and what you need." He chuckled. "Stop trying to pretend you don't want this."

"I saw the way your … friends looked at us in that nightclub, Alonzo. They weren't happy to see us."

"I don't care what they want or wanted. I'm with you, and that's the way it's going to stay."

"But don't you have to follow some kind of protocol or something like that?" she asked.

"I don't have to follow anything I don't want. I told you, Tessa. I'm the master of my own destiny, and you need to see that I'm not going to back down without a fight. I love you more than anything else in this world. If they push me aside, tell me I'm not fit to run the Zanetti name, then they can take over. Believe me, it wouldn't last long before they came my way. That is a promise."

She smiled up at him.

"I love you, Tessa. These feelings are not going away, and I would never dream of asking you to become something that you have no right. You're going to be my wife. The mother of my children."

"Where is that son of mine?"

The loud screech filled the air and echoed off all the walls.

Tessa stared at the surprise on Alonzo's face, and then he began to chuckle. "They have brought reinforcements. You're about to meet my mother."

Before she could form any kind of excuse the door slammed open, and in walked a force to be reckoned with.

His mother, Maria Zanetti, with a glare that would kill most people on the spot.

Tessa's heart raced. She tried to step away from Alonzo, but he wrapped an arm around her waist, stopping her from escaping.

It wasn't fair as he had the advantage like always. Gritting her teeth, she stayed perfectly still.

"You think you can take over the name and just start making all the rules," Maria asked, her hands waving at her son.

"Hello, Mother, what a pleasant surprise to see you back here."

"You knew I would come. No matter what happened, I was going to turn up. Your father may have angered me during his dying breath, but that was no reason for me not to return here when I hear you're making a mockery of my name by marrying this, this peasant."

Alonzo tensed behind her. He still didn't let her go.

"I suggest you be careful, Mother. I'm very much in love with this ... peasant. She is going to be my wife."

"She is a soldier's daughter. You think I don't know what has been happening here. First, you allow this witch to attack my son-in-law, then you—"

"That son-in-law was beating the living shit out of your daughter."

"Enough, Alonzo. You know not to interfere with a couple's marriage."

"Interfere? You were fucking pissed that Dad organized it. You didn't want Jessica to marry into the family or to be part of the Adesso. You've been sulking since his death because he didn't grant you that one wish. Don't you dare come in here and tell me you supported it when you've not even seen your grandson."

"The same grandson that she has been taking care of."

"Who is the mole in my household?" Alonzo asked.

"Don't worry. You already fired her. I've been paying her to keep a watch on everything."

Alonzo laughed. "You paid a whore to do a proper job. You should have just asked me. Was that so hard? To call your son and to find out what was going on in the family you left behind. In the family you neglected."

"I did not neglect you."

"You certainly didn't stick around to help it. I've been doing the best I can with the fuck-up you and Father created."

"And you think marrying this girl is going to help that? You cannot marry her. The only person you can marry now is an Acquati. Their oldest daughter. It will cement your future. She'll give you good sons."

"I'm not marrying her, Mother."

"You will."

"I'm marrying Tessa Brown, and that is final. You want to test me on this, go ahead. I have already started the proceedings." Alonzo placed a hand on her stomach. "And there may already be a child here."

His mother gasped. "You wouldn't."

"Oh, believe me I would. You think I didn't know what was at risk with all of this? I knew, and I was ready to face the consequences. You want to kick me out, take this title from me, be my guest. I'm the only one who knows all the secrets of the Zanetti." Alonzo kissed her shoulder. "Go and find Jessica. I'm going to deal with my mother."

Tessa didn't mind leaving. Arguments were never something she enjoyed being part of.

She found Jessica out in the garden like she did most days with Caesar.

The moment she approached, Jessica smiled. "How are things going with Mother?"

"I think she hates me."

"Of course she does. She promised me I'd never get married to anyone I couldn't stand. Dad forced me to marry Benedict, and Mother showed she had no power. Her only true grip was trying to do the same to Alonzo. It would have been her easiest way of getting back at Dad for not listening to her." Jessica shrugged. "Alonzo can handle her."

She watched as Jessica blew on Caesar's stomach. The little boy started to giggle, and she was so happy for the two of them.

Resting her hand on her stomach, she thought about Maria's reaction to Alonzo's ... threat. It sounded like a threat.

"Can I ask you something?" Tessa asked.

"Of course. I don't know if I'll be able to answer it."

"Alonzo touched my stomach and said to your mother there could be a child here already. She looked mortified. Why?"

Jessica smiled. "My brother is sly. The men in our world, they cannot get anyone pregnant but their wife."

"There can't be a guarantee with that, Jessica. No one can."

"In our world, if a woman who is the mistress or the whore of one of our men and she gets pregnant." Jessica stopped, and Tessa's heart pounded. "She's not allowed to keep it."

"That can't be possible."

"They're too much of a liability, and they can't be allowed to have children. Benedict told me that some of the women have their tubes tied to prevent it."

"That's awful. What if they want children when that guy decides he doesn't want her?"

Jessica shrugged. "I don't think they're allowed to, you know, have anyone outside of our world. They have to stay part of the families in some way, and so they get passed around."

"Wow, that is so awful."

"I know, but that's the rules and the way they are."

"I don't think I could stand to do that."

"It's not a good life, Tessa. Are you sure you want to marry my brother?"

"I know I love him."

"Is that enough?" Jessica asked.

Tessa placed a hand on her stomach. "I don't know if I'm pregnant or not. I don't want to get rid of it."

"I think what you need to realize, Tessa, if you can't stand this life, I do truly believe Alonzo would walk away. He'd leave all of this behind for you."

"But this is his world."

"You mean a lot more to him than a name. I've seen my brother with women over the years. Never have I seen him pursue a woman the way he does you. It's like he doesn't even see straight. You're the only one he wants."

Suddenly a loud bang filled the air, followed by several more.

Jessica grabbed Caesar, and they turned in the direction of the noise.

Benedict had just shot three of the guards and was heading their way.

Fear gripped Tessa.

Jessica and Caesar were both here, and she couldn't let anything happen to them.

****

"Alonzo, my son, you know this is not the way our world works," Maria said. "You cannot marry that girl."

He stared at his mother and shook his head. "Do you know what is funny? You thinking you have any control over me or what I do."

"Look, she seems like a nice girl. I remember her father well. I do. Keep her. Put her to one side and do what all men do. Have a woman that you will enjoy to visit that you can use. But don't put the family at risk like this. Do not do that."

"Do you think I don't know what you're all about?" Alonzo asked. "You think I don't know about how pissed you were at Dad because he didn't take your last request seriously? You didn't want Jessica to marry into the Adesso, but he organized it anyway. You want to ruin my happiness because you have some twisted view in thinking that you know what you're doing. You don't have a fucking clue, Mother. You left this house. You have no power here. Tessa Brown will be my wife. Our children will be your grandkids, and mark my words, right here, right now, if you treat her with anything but the utmost respect, I will make sure you never come back here again, do you understand me?"

"You'd threaten your mother over this girl?"

"Mom, you need to understand that I would move heaven and fucking hell for this girl. I have loved her for a long time. She wasn't ready to know how much, but I cannot let her go. There's no way I can have second best with her. She is my number one."

"It's not going to be easy. Your enemies will know the truth. She'll be easy to find."

"I've got the best men to protect her. She will want for nothing and will live a long life."

The sound of bullets firing filled the air.

Maria screamed as the office door slammed open.

"Benedict's on the land. He's killed five men already. He has Jessica, Caesar, and Tessa," a guard said.

Alonzo was already at his drawer, pulling out his gun and his knife.

"Stay here." He gave the order to his mother.

Leaving the office, he walked by the kitchen. Louise was cowering in the corner.

"He just shot them in the head. Didn't care they were men with families. Just shot them," Louise said.

He nodded at Cole to get her the hell out of there.

Alonzo should have known Benedict would come back. He'd taken everything from the woman-beating fucker. He'd been cast out. Once his father knew the true extent of Benedict's dealings with the human traffickers, all hell had broken out. Adesso had disowned his only son and was now trying to find a suitable partner for his daughter who would be able to take his place.

Everything was fucked up, and it was all because of that fucker's greed. It pissed him off.

Standing toward the door, he stared out the window, being careful not to be seen. Benedict stood with a gun pointed at Tessa. Jessica and Caesar were nowhere to be seen.

He couldn't have this man standing over his woman.

Stepping out of the door, he started to advance toward Benedict.

"I suggest you stop right there, Alonzo," Benedict said.

"You're on my land, pointing a gun at my woman. Who the fuck do you think you are?" He wanted Benedict to turn that gun on him.

"I want Jessica, and I want Caesar. They are mine."

"They are not yours. You're not even an Adesso anymore."

"That was your fucking fault. You should have done what I told you to do. There's money to be made in flesh, Alonzo. By bringing yourself close to—"

"Enough," Alonzo said.

"You know what, you're right. Let's see how you like having something you care about taken away from you."

Benedict fired his gun, and Alonzo didn't hesitate. He fired his own weapon. Benedict's head exploded, and he fell to the ground.

Rushing to Tessa's side, he cupped her face.

The expression he saw scared him.

"Baby, baby, I've got you. I've got you."

"Alonzo," she said.

He wrapped his arms around her, hugging her tightly. "Fuck, baby, I love you so damn much. We're getting married wherever you want to marry. I don't care. I love you."

"I love you, Alonzo, so much."

Suddenly, she became really heavy, and he held her tightly.

Jessica and Caesar came out from behind a statue.

He stared down at Tessa as he lowered her to the ground. She'd not been holding him back. Her hands had been covering her stomach.

He pulled her hands away and saw the blood soaking her shirt.

"Shit!" He lifted up her shirt and saw the wound seeping blood. "Get an ambulance. A doctor. Any fucking thing. Just … make it stop." He removed his shirt, pressing it against the wound. "You're fine, Tessa. Honey, you're fine."

She nodded her head, and he saw the pain in her eyes. She was trying to hide it.

"I love you, Alonzo. I don't care about anything else. I would have been a good wife to you." She talked slowly.

He heard the commotion going on around him, but he ignored it all.

"You will make a good life for me, babe. We're going to be so happy. We're going to go away. I'll take you all over the world, to every single beach your heart desires. You'll want for nothing. We're going to have a lot of children. We'll name them after each letter of the alphabet."

Tessa laughed and cried out.

"You just can't leave me, Tessa. You hear me? I love you so damn much. You can't leave me."

"I don't ever want to leave you. I love you."

He leaned down, and even as his hands were covered in her blood, he cupped her face, kissing her back with a passion. "Don't leave me. I forbid you from leaving me."

He didn't know how much time had passed or what was happening.

This woman, he loved her more than anything.

"Alonzo, the ambulance is here," Cole said.

He stayed by her side as the two men loaded her onto a gurney. They were already working on her, opening up her shirt to reveal the wound.

Jessica was crying as she held onto Caesar. His mother had come out, and his men were there.

Alonzo didn't give a shit though. Tears fell down his cheeks, and he was in agony as he watched the only person he had ever loved get wheeled away.

He followed her.

"No, Alonzo, don't. One of the men will go with her," Maria said.

His mother held his arm. When he was a boy, he would have listened to her.

He would have listened to his father and done what was required of him. He watched Tessa's feet disappear around the corner of the house.

Turning to his mother, he glared at her. Pulling his gun out of his pants, he pressed it against her forehead. She looked completely startled but he didn't care. "Let's get something clear, right here, right now. That woman is my life. She is my fucking reason for breathing. You will not keep me from her. You will never keep us apart, and I will turn this entire fucking city into a bloodbath. Test me, Mother, and you'll be the one dead."

He moved away from her and rushed around the building just as the doors were about to close.

"She's my fiancée. I'm coming with you." He climbed into the back of the ambulance.

Tessa was no longer conscious. He held her hand, hating that her blood covered his. The men kept working, and he just sat there and did something he'd not done in a long time. He prayed.

In a world like his that was full of darkness and fear, he prayed to whoever was listening and hoped that someone cared enough.

She was too good to be gone, to have her life taken from her.

Even as the tears fell from his eyes, he stayed with her.

When they got to the hospital, one of the men put a hand on his stomach. He couldn't follow her into surgery. The bullet was still in her stomach, and they had to operate.

Jessica, Caesar, Cole, and Demetri arrived as he was filling out her medical forms. They were not an issue for him as he'd been taking care of her for a long time now.

"If she doesn't make it," Alonzo said. "I will declare war on Adesso and his entire fucking clan."

"Alonzo, you know he acted alone," Jessica said.

"I don't give a fuck. His father should have had him on a leash. He came into my home. Killed my men and attacked my woman. That is not going to go away lightly." He rubbed at his eyes.

"Alonzo, don't react. Not yet. Not until you know what is going to happen," Jessica said. "She's a fighter, and you're going to see that."

He sat back, staring at the door he'd seen her

being taken through. If she died today, he would cause pain and terror unlike anything the world had ever seen. He would kill, torture, and make people fear the name Tessa Brown as he avenged her death. Then, once his job was done, he would follow her because his life was worth nothing without her.

Epilogue

Six months later

Tessa moaned as Alonzo filled her pussy. His body covered hers. Their fingers were locked together as he rode her, their wedding bands catching her eye as he kissed her neck.

She was so turned on by the man that was now her husband.

Her recovery from getting shot had been a huge success. The bullet had entered her stomach, and the removal of it hadn't been too difficult. The longest part of her recovery was waiting for the hole to heal. She ended on up a restricted diet so she wouldn't cause further damage.

Throughout it all, Alonzo was by her side. The moment she made it out of the hospital a month later—he wouldn't let her leave sooner and had given the hospital a huge donation—they'd gotten married. Jessica had helped her to arrange it all from her hospital bed. The gown, the church, all of it had been so magical, but what made it more so was knowing Alonzo would be waiting for her.

The instant she entered the church and saw him, all of her worries had faded away and all that remained was the two of them.

Maria hadn't stayed with them. Alonzo had told her she'd made a permanent move to Italy.

Jessica and Caesar lived with them, and Tessa helped out as often as she could.

With regards to Alonzo and dealing with the other members of the mafia, they hadn't refused to acknowledge him. He was still the leader of the Zanetti family, his role within the mafia still there. There were times she was nervous for him. Whenever he had to leave to exact justice or to deal with problems that came his way, she feared for his life.

She had washed many of his clothes that were covered in blood.

Still, she wouldn't back down.

He was the love of her life, and as he wrapped his arms around her, she smiled.

"Alonzo," she said, moaning as his hand moved between her thighs, teasing her clit.

"I love it when your pussy tightens around me. It feels so fucking good."

"I'm pregnant," she said.

This made him pause. "What?"

"I'm pregnant We're going to have a baby."

He pulled out of her and rolled her onto her back. "We're going to have a baby?" He stroked her abdomen.

"I took a test this morning. It was positive. I've booked an appointment to see the doctor. They can confirm it."

"Oh, fuck, I can't wait, baby. You're going to be the best damn mother in the world." He gripped the back of her neck, drawing her closer for a kiss.

She kissed him back and moaned. "And you're going to be one hell of a dad." She stroked his cheek. "I love you, Alonzo."

"You're the best fucking thing to ever happen to me."

Jessica had told her how scared he was when she'd been taken into surgery. Not a moment had gone by when she didn't know how much he loved her. He told her every day, showed her more love than she ever thought was possible, and no matter what, he owned her heart.

"Now make love to me, Alonzo. Like you mean it." She winked at him, and he growled, pressing her against the bed.

"We're not leaving this bed ever again."

"I sure hope not."

The End

www.samcrescent.com

BESTSELLING BBW ROMANCE
SPICY ROMANCE FOR REAL WOMEN